CLOSE EN
THE WORST KIND

One of the crew came forth. Great God, how shall I describe the horror of that first sight? Surely, my mind shrieked, this was a demon from the lowest pits of hell.

He stood about five feet tall, very broad and powerful, clad in a tunic of silvery sheen. His skin was hairless and deep blue. He had a short thick tail. The ears were long and pointed on either side of his round head; narrow amber eyes glared from a blunt-snouted face; but his brow was high.

Someone began to scream. Red John brandished his bow. "Quiet, there!" he roared. " 'Steeth, I'll kill the first man who moves!"

I hardly thought this a time for profanity. Raising the cross still higher, I forced limp legs to carry me a few steps forward, while I quavered some chant of exorcism. I was certain it would do no good; the end of the world was upon us.

Had the demon only remained standing there, we would soon have broken and bolted. But he raised a tube held in one hand. From it shot flame, blinding white. I heard it crackle in the air and saw a man near me smitten. Fire burst over him. He fell dead, his breast charred open.

Three other demons emerged.

Soldiers were trained to react when such things happened, not to think. The bow of Red John sang. The foremost demon lurched off the ramp with a cloth-yard arrow through him. I saw him cough blood and die. As if the one shot had touched off a hundred, the air was suddenly gray with whistling shafts. The three other demons toppled, so thickly studded with arrows they might have been popinjays at a contest.

"They can be slain!" bawled Sir Roger. "Haro! St. George for merry England!" And he spurred his horse straight up the gangway. With one crazed whoop the whole army charged after him.

THE HIGH CRUSADE

POUL ANDERSON

BAEN BOOKS

THE HIGH CRUSADE

This is a work of fiction. All the characters and events portrayed in this book are fictional, and any resemblance to real people or incidents is purely coincidental.

A Baen Book

Baen Publishing Enterprises
P.O. Box 1403
Riverdale, N.Y. 10471

ISBN: 0-671-72074-0

Cover art by Darrell Sweet

First Baen printing, August 1991

Distributed by
SIMON & SCHUSTER
1230 Avenue of the Americas
New York, N.Y. 10020

Printed in the United States of America

To JENS CHRISTIAN and
NANCY HOSTRUP—
as well as PER and JANNE—
gratefully and hopefully

Prologue

As the captain looked up, the hooded desk lamp threw his face into ridges of darkness and craggy highlights. A port stood open to alien summer night.

"Well?" he said.

"I've got it translated, sir," answered the sociotechnician. "Had to extrapolate backward from modern languages, which is what took me so long. In the course of the work, though, I've learned enough so I can talk to these ... creatures."

"Good," grunted the captain. "Now maybe we can discover what this is all about. Thunder and blowup! I expected to come across almost anything out here, but this—!"

"I know how you feel, sir. Even with all the physical evidence right before my eyes, I found it hard to believe the original account."

"Very well, I'll read it at once. No rest for the wicked." The captain nodded dismissal, and the socio-tech departed the cabin.

1

For a moment the captain sat motionless, looking at the document but not really seeing it. The book itself had been impressively ancient, uncials on vellum between massive covers. This translation was a prosaic typescript. Yet he was nearly afraid to turn the pages, afraid of what he might find out. There had been some stupendous catastrophe, more than a thousand years ago; its consequences were still echoing. The captain felt very small and alone. Home was a long ways off.

However . . .

He began to read.

Chapter I

Archbishop William, a most learned and holy prelate, having commanded me to put into English writing those great events to which I was a humble witness, I take up my quill in the name of the Lord and my patron saint: trusting that they will aid my feeble powers of narrative for the sake of future generations who may with profit study the account of Sir Roger de Tourneville's campaign and learn thereby fervently to reverence the great God by Whom all things are brought to pass.

I shall write of these happenings exactly as I remember them, without fear or favor, the more so since most who were concerned are now dead. I myself was quite insignificant, but since it is well to make known the chronicler that men may judge his trustworthiness, let me first say a few words about him.

I was born forty years before my story begins, a younger son of Wat Brown. He was blacksmith in the little town of Ansby, which lay in northeastern Lincolnshire. The lands were enfeoffed to the Baron de Tourneville, whose ancient castle stood on a hill just above the town. There was also a small abbey of the Franciscan order, which I entered as a boy. Having gained some skill (my only skill, I fear) in reading and writing, I was often made instructor in these arts to novices and the children of lay people. My boyhood nickname I put into Latin and made my religious one, as a lesson in humility, so I am Brother Parvus. For I am of low size, and ill-favored, though fortunate to have the trust of children.

In the year of grace 1345, Sir Roger, then baron, was gathering an army of free companions to join our puissant King Edward III and his son in the French war. Ansby was the meeting place. By May Day, the army was all there. It camped on the common, but turned our quiet town into one huge brawl. Archers, crossbowmen, pikemen, and cavalry swarmed through the muddy streets, drinking, gaming, wenching, jesting, and quarreling, to the peril of their souls and our thatch-roofed cottages. Indeed, we lost two houses to fire. Yet they brought in unwonted ardor, a sense of glory, such that the very serfs thought wistfully about going along, were it but possible. Even I entertained such notions. For me it might well have come true, for I had been tutoring Sir Roger's son and had also brought his accounts in order. The baron talked of making me his amanuensis; but my abbot was doubtful.

Thus it stood when the Wersgor ship arrived.

Well I remember the day. I was out on an errand. The weather had turned sunny after rain, the town street was ankle-deep in mud. I picked my way through the aimless crowds of soldiery, nodding to such as I knew. All at once a great cry arose. I lifted my head like the others.

Lo! It was as a miracle! Down through the sky, seeming to swell monstrously with the speed of its descent, came a ship all of metal. So dazzling was the sunlight off its polished sides that I could not see its form clearly. A huge cylinder, I thought, easily two thousand feet long. Save for the whistle of wind, it moved noiseless.

Someone screamed. A woman knelt in a puddle and began to rattle off prayers. A man cried that his sins had found him out, and joined her. Worthy though these actions were, I realized that in such a mass of people, folk would be trampled to death if panic smote. That was surely not what God, if He had sent this visitant, intended.

Hardly knowing what I did, I sprang up on a great iron bombard whose wagon was sunk to the axles in our street. "Hold fast!" I cried. "Be not afraid! Have faith and hold fast!"

My feeble pipings went unheard. Then Red John Hameward, the captain of the longbowmen, leaped up beside me. A merry giant, with hair like spun copper and fierce blue eyes, he had been my friend since he arrived here.

"I know not what yon thing is," he bellowed. His voice rolled over the general babble, which died away. "Mayhap some French trick. Or it may be friendly, which would make our fear look all the sillier. Follow me, every soldier, to meet it when it lands!"

"Magic!" cried an old man. " 'Tis sorcery, and we are undone!"

"Not so," I told him. "Sorcery cannot harm good Christians."

"But I am a miserable sinner," he wailed.

"St. George and King Edward!" Red John sprang off the tube and dashed down the street. I tucked up my robe and panted after him, trying to remember the formulas of exorcism.

Looking back over my shoulder, I was surprised to see most of the company follow us. They had not so much taken heart from the bowman's example, as they were afraid to be left leaderless. But they followed—into their own camp to snatch weapons, then out onto the common. I saw that cavalrymen had flung themselves to horse and were thundering downhill from the castle.

Sir Roger de Tourneville, unarmored but wearing sword at hip, led the riders. He shouted and flailed about with his lance. Between them, he and Red John got the rabble whipped into some kind of fighting order. They had scarcely finished when the great ship landed.

It sank deep into pasture earth; its weight was tremendous, and I knew not what had borne it so lightly through the air. I saw that it was all enclosed, a smooth shell without poop deck or forecastle. I did not really expect oars, but part of me wondered (through the hammering of my heart) why there were no sails. However, I did spy turrets, from which poked muzzles like those of bombards.

There fell a shuddering silence. Sir Roger edged his horse up to me where I stood with teeth clapping in my head. "You're a learned cleric, Brother Parvus," he said quietly, though his nostrils were white and his hair dank with sweat. "What d'you make of this?"

"In truth I know not, sire," I stammered. "Ancient stories tell of wizards like Merlin who could fly through the air."

"Could it be . . . divine?" He crossed himself.

" 'Tis not for me to say." I looked timidly skyward. "Yet I see no choir of angels."

A muted clank came from the vessel, drowned in one groan of fear as a circular door began to open. But all stood their ground, being Englishmen, if not simply too terrified to run.

I glimpsed that the door was double, with a chamber between. A metallic ramp slid forth like a tongue, three yards downward until it touched the earth. I raised my crucifix while Aves pattered from my lips like hail.

One of the crew came forth. Great God, how shall I describe the horror of that first sight? Surely, my mind shrieked, this was a demon from the lowest pits of hell.

He stood about five feet tall, very broad and powerful, clad in a tunic of silvery sheen. His skin was hairless and deep blue. He had a short thick tail. The ears were long and pointed on either side of his round head; narrow amber eyes glared from a blunt-snouted face; but his brow was high.

Someone began to scream. Red John brandished his bow. "Quiet, there!" he roared. "'Steeth, I'll kill the first man who moves!"

I hardly thought this a time for profanity. Raising the cross still higher, I forced limp legs to carry me a few steps forward, while I quavered some chant of exorcism. I was certain it would do no good; the end of the world was upon us.

Had the demon only remained standing there, we would soon have broken and bolted. But he raised a tube held in one hand. From it shot flame, blinding white. I heard it crackle in the air and saw a man near me smitten. Fire burst over him. He fell dead, his breast charred open.

Three other demons emerged.

Soldiers were trained to react when such things happened, not to think. The bow of Red John sang. The foremost demon lurched off the ramp with a cloth-yard arrow through him. I saw him cough blood and die. As if the one shot had touched off a hundred, the air was suddenly gray with whistling shafts. The three other demons toppled, so thickly studded with arrows they might have been popinjays at a contest.

"They can be slain!" bawled Sir Roger. "Haro! St. George for merry England!" And he spurred his horse straight up the gangway.

They say fear breeds unnatural courage. With one crazed whoop the whole army charged after him. Be it confessed, I, too, howled and ran into the ship.

Of that combat which ramped and raged through all the rooms and corridors, I have little memory. Somewhere, from someone, I got a battle-ax. There is in me a confused impression of smiting away at vile blue faces which rose up to snarl at me, of slipping in blood and rising to smite again. Sir Roger had no way to direct the battle. His men simply ran wild. Knowing the demons could be killed, their one thought was to kill and have done.

The crew of the ship numbered about a hundred, but few carried weapons. We later found all manner of devices stored in the holds, but the invaders had relied on creating a panic. Not knowing Englishmen, they had not expected trouble. The ship's artillery was ready to use, but of no value once we were inside.

In less than an hour, we had hunted them all down.

Wading out through the carnage, I wept with joy to feel the blessed sunlight again. Sir Roger was checking with his captains to find our losses, which were only fifteen all told. As I stood there, atremble with exhaustion, Red John Hameward emerged. He had a demon slung over his shoulder.

He threw the creature at Sir Roger's feet. "This one I knocked out with my fist, sire," he panted. "I thought might be you'd want one kept alive awhile, to put him to the question. Or should I not take chances, and slice off his ugly head now?"

Sir Roger considered. Calm had descended upon him; none of us had yet grasped the enormity of this event. A grim smile crossed his lips. He replied in English as fluent as the nobleman's French he more commonly used.

"If these be demons," he said, "they're a poor breed, for they were slain as easily as men. Easier, in sooth. They didn't know more about infighting than my little daughter. Less, for she's given my nose many hefty tweaks. I think chains will hold this fellow safe, eh, Brother Parvus?"

"Yes, my lord," I opined, "though it were best to put some saints' relics and the Host near by."

"Well, then, take him to the abbey and see what you can get out of him. I'll send a guard along. Come up to dinner this evening."

"Sire," I reproved, "we should hold a great Mass of thanksgiving ere we do anything else."

"Yes, yes," he said impatiently. "Talk to your abbot about it. Do what seems best. But come to dinner and tell me what you've learned."

His eyes grew thoughtful as he stared at the ship.

Chapter II

I came as ordered, with the approval of my abbot, who saw that here the ghostly and secular arms must be one. The town was strangely quiet as I picked my way through sunset streets. Folk were in church or huddled within doors. From the soldiers' camp I could hear yet another Mass. The ship brooded mountainous over all our tiny works.

But we felt heartened, I believe, a little drunk with our success over powers not of this earth. The smug conclusion seemed inescapable, that God approved of us.

I passed the bailey through a trebled watch and went directly to the great hall. Ansby Castle was old Norman work, gaunt to look on, cold to inhabit. The hall was already dark, lit by candles and a great leaping fire which picked weapons and tapestries out of unrestful shadow. Gentlefolk and the more important commoners of town and army were at table, a buzz of talk, servants scurrying about, dogs lolling on the

rushes. It was a comfortingly familiar scene, however
much tension underlay it. Sir Roger beckoned me to
come sit with him and his lady, a signal honor.

Let me here describe Roger de Tourneville, knight
and baron. He was a big, strongly thewed man of
thirty years, with gray eyes and bony curve-nosed features. He wore his yellow hair in the usual style of a
warrior peer, thick on the crown and shaven below—
which somewhat marred an otherwise not unhandsome
appearance, for he had ears like jug handles. This, his
home district, was poor and backward, and most of
his time elsewhere had been spent in war. So he
lacked courtly graces, though shrewd and kindly in his
fashion. His wife, Lady Catherine, was a daughter of
the Viscount de Mornay; most people felt she had
married beneath her style of living as well as her station, for she had been brought up at Winchester
amidst every elegance and modern refinement. She
was very beautiful, with great blue eyes and auburn
hair, but somewhat of a virago. They had only two
children: Robert, a fine boy of six, who was my pupil,
and a three-year-old girl named Matilda.

"Well, Brother Parvus," boomed my lord. "Sit
down. Have a stoup of wine—'sblood, this occasion
calls for more than ale!" Lady Catherine's delicate
nose wrinkled a bit; in her old home, ale was only
for commoners. When I was seated, Sir Roger leaned
forward and said intently, "What have you found out?
Is it a demon we've captured?"

A hush fell over the table. Even the dogs were
quiet. I could hear the hearth fire crackle and ancient
banners stir dustily where they hung from the beams
overhead. "I think so, my lord," I answered with care,
"for he grew very angry when we sprinkled holy water
on him."

"Yet he did not vanish in a puff of smoke? Hah! If
demons, these are not kin to any I ever heard of.
They're mortal as men."

"More so, sire," declared one of his captains, "for they cannot have souls."

"I'm not interested in their blithering souls," snorted Sir Roger. "I want to know about their ship. I've walked through it since the fight. What a by-our-lady whale of a ship! We could put all Ansby aboard, with room to spare. Did you ask the demon why a mere hundred of 'em needed that much space?"

"He does not speak any known language, my lord," I said.

"Nonsense! All demons know Latin, at least. He's just being stubborn."

"Mayhap a little session with your executioner?" asked the knight Sir Owain Montbelle slyly.

"No," I said. "If it please you, best not. He seems very quick at learning. Already he repeats many words after me, so I do not believe he is merely pretending ignorance. Give me a few days and I may be able to talk with him."

"A few days may be too much," grumbled Sir Roger. He threw the beef bone he had been gnawing to the dogs and licked his fingers noisily. Lady Catherine frowned and pointed to the water bowl and napkin before him. "I'm sorry, my sweet," he muttered. "I never can remember about these newfangled things."

Sir Owain delivered him from his embarrassment by inquiring: "Why say you a few days may be too long? Surely you are not expecting another ship?"

"No. But the men will be more restless than ever. We were almost ready to depart, and now *this* happens!"

"So? Can we not leave anyhow on the date planned?"

"No, you blockhead!" Sir Roger's fist landed on the table. A goblet jumped. "Cannot you see what a chance this is? It must have been given us by the saints themselves!"

As we sat awestruck, he went on rapidly: "We can take the whole company aboard that thing. Horses, cows, pigs, fowls—we'll not be deviled by supply problems. Women, too, all the comforts of home! Aye, why not even the children? Never mind the crops hereabouts, they can stand neglect for a while and 'tis safer to keep everyone together lest there should be another visitation.

"I know not what powers the ship owns besides flying, but her very appearance will strike such terror we'll scarce need to fight. So we'll take her across the Channel and end the French war inside a month, d' you see? Then we go on and liberate the Holy Land, and get back here in time for hay harvest!"

A long silence ended abruptly in such a storm of cheers that my own weak protests were drowned out. I thought the scheme altogether mad. So, I could see, did Lady Catherine and a few others. But the rest were laughing and shouting till the hall roared.

Sir Roger turned a flushed face to me. "It depends on you, Brother Parvus," he said. "You're the best of us all in matters of language. You must make the demon talk, or teach him how, whichever it is. He's got to show us how to sail that ship!"

"My noble lord—" I quavered.

"Good!" Sir Roger slapped my back so I choked and nearly fell off my seat. "I knew you could do it. Your reward will be the privilege of coming with us!"

Indeed, it was as if the town and the army were alike possessed. Surely the one wise course was to send messages posthaste to the bishop, perhaps to Rome itself, begging counsel. But no, they must all go, at once. Wives would not leave their husbands, or parents their children, or girls their lovers. The lowliest serf looked up from his acre and dreamed of freeing the Holy Land and picking up a coffer of gold on the way.

What else can be expected of a folk bred from Saxon, Dane, and Norman?

I returned to the abbey and spent the night on my

knees, praying for a sign. But the saints remained non-committal. After matins I went with a heavy heart to my abbot and told him what the baron had commanded. He was wroth at not being allowed immediate communication with the Church authorities but decided it was best we obey for the nonce. I was released from other duties that I might study how to converse with the demon.

I girded myself and went down to the cell where he was confined. It was a narrow room, half underground, used for penances. Brother Thomas, our smith, had stapled fetters to the walls and chained the creature up. He lay on a straw pallet, a frightful sight in the gloom. His links clashed as he rose at my entry. Our relics in their chests were placed near by, just out of his impious reach, so that the thighbone of St. Osbert and the sixth-year molar of St. Willibald might keep him from bursting his bonds and escaping back to hell.

Though I would not have been at all sorry had he done so.

I crossed myself and squatted down. His yellow eyes glared at me. I had brought paper, ink, and quills, to exercise what small talent I have for drawing. I sketched a man and said, "*Homo*," for it seemed wiser to teach him Latin than any language confined to a single nation. Then I drew another man and showed him that the two were called *homines*. Thus it went, and he was quick to learn.

Presently he signaled for the paper, and I gave it to him. He himself drew skillfully. He told me that his name was *Branithar* and that his race was called *Wersgorix*. I was unable to find these terms in any demonology. But thereafter I let him guide our studies, for his race had made the learning of new languages into a science, and our task went apace.

I worked long hours with him and saw little of the outside world in the next few days. Sir Roger kept his domain incommunicado. I think his greatest fear was that some earl or duke might seize the ship for himself. With his bolder men, the baron spent much time aboard it, trying to fathom all the wonders he encountered.

Erelong Branithar was able to complain about the bread-and-water diet and threaten revenge. I was still afraid of him but kept up a bold front. Of course, our conversation was much slower than I here render it, with many pauses while we searched for words.

"You brought this on yourself," I told him. "You should have known better than to make an unprovoked attack on Christians."

"What are Christians?" he asked.

Dumfounded, I thought he must be feigning ignorance. As a test, I led him through the Paternoster. He did not go up in smoke, which puzzled me.

"I think I understand," he said. "You refer to some primitive tribal pantheon."

"It is no such heathen thing!" I said indignantly. I started to explain the Trinity to him, but had scarcely gotten to transubstantiation when he waved an impatient blue hand. It was much like a human hand otherwise, save for the thick, sharp nails.

"No matter," he said. "Are all Christians as ferocious as your people?"

"You would have had better luck with the French," I admitted. "Your misfortune was landing among Englishmen."

"A stubborn breed," he nodded. "It will cost you dearly. But if you release me at once, I will try to mitigate the vengeance which is going to fall on you."

My tongue clove to the roof of my mouth, but I unstuck it and asked him coolly enough to elucidate. Whence came he, and what were his intentions?

That took a long time for him to make clear, because the very concepts were strange. I thought surely he was lying, but at least he acquired more Latin in the process.

It was about two weeks after the landing when Sir Owain Montbelle appeared at the abbey and demanded audience with me. I met him in the cloister garden; we found a bench and sat down.

This Owain was the younger son, by a second marriage with a Welsh woman, of a petty baron on the Marches. I daresay the ancient conflict of two nations smoldered strangely in his breast; but the Cymric charm was also there. Made page and later esquire to a great knight in the royal court, young Owain had captured his master's heart and been brought up with all the privilege of far higher ranks. He had traveled widely abroad, become a troubadour of some note, received the accolade—and then suddenly, there he was, penniless. In hopes of winning his fortune, he had wandered to Ansby to join the free companions. Though valiant enough, he was too darkly handsome for most men's taste, and they said no husband felt safe when he was about. This was not quite true, for Sir Roger had taken a fancy to the youth, admired his judgment as well as his education, and was happy that at last Lady Catherine had someone to talk to about the things that most interested her.

"I come from my lord, Brother Parvus," Sir Owain began. "He wishes to know how much longer you will need to tame this beast of ours."

"Oh . . . he speaks glibly enough now," I answered. "But he holds so firmly to out-and-out falsehoods that I have not yet thought it worth while to report."

"Sir Roger grows most impatient, and the men can scarcely be held any longer. They devour his substance, and not a night passes without a brawl or a murder. We must start soon or not at all."

"Then I beg you not to go," I said. "Not in yon ship out of hell." I could see that dizzyingly tall spire, its nose wreathed with low clouds, rearing beyond the abbey walls. It terrified me.

"Well," snapped Sir Owain, "what has the monster told you?"

"He has the impudence to claim he comes not from below, but from above. From heaven itself!"

"He . . . an angel?"

"No. He says he is neither angel nor demon, but a member of another mortal race than mankind."

Sir Owain caressed his smooth-shaven chin with one hand. "It could be," he mused. "After all, if Unipeds and Centaurs and other monstrous beings exist, why not those squatty blueskins?"

"I know. Twould be reasonable enough, save that he claims to live in the sky."

"Tell me just what he did say."

"As you will, Sir Owain, but remember that these impieties are not mine. This Branithar insists that the earth is not flat but is a sphere hanging in space. Nay, he goes further and says the earth moves about the sun! Some of the learned ancients held similar notions, but I cannot understand what would keep the oceans from pouring off into space or—"

"Pray continue the story, Brother Parvus."

"Well, Branithar says that the stars are other suns than ours, only very far off, and have worlds going about them even as our own does. Not even the Greeks could have swallowed such an absurdity. What kind of ignorant yokels does the creature take us for? But be this as it may, Branithar says that his people, the Wersgorix, come from one of these other worlds, one which is much like our earth. He boasts of their powers of sorcery—"

"That much is no lie," said Sir Owain. "We've been trying out some of those hand weapons. We burned down three houses, a pig, and a serf ere we learned how to control them."

I gulped, but went on: "These Wersgorix have ships which can fly between the stars. They have conquered many worlds. Their method is to subdue or wipe out any backward natives there may be. Then they settle the entire world, each Wersgor taking hundreds of thousands of acres. Their numbers are growing so fast, and they so dislike being crowded, that they must ever be seeking new worlds.

"This ship we captured was a scout, exploring in search of another place to conquer. Having observed our earth from above, they decided it was suitable for their use and descended. Their plan was the usual one, which had never failed them hitherto. They would terrorize us, use our home as a base, and range about gathering specimens of plants, animals, and minerals. That is the reason their ship is so big, with so much empty space. 'Twas to be a veritable Noah's ark. When they returned home and reported their findings, a fleet would come to attack all mankind."

"Hm," said Sir Owain. "We stopped that much, at least."

We were both cushioned against the frightful vision of our poor folk being harried by unhumans, destroyed or enslaved, because neither of us really believed it. I had decided that Branithar came from a distant part of the world, perhaps beyond Cathay, and only told these lies in the hope of frightening us into letting him go. Sir Owain agreed with my theory.

"Nonetheless," added the knight, "we must certainly learn to use the ship, lest more of them arrive. And what better way to learn, than by taking it to France and Jerusalem? As my lord said, 'twould in that case be prudent as well as comfortable to have women, children, yeomen, and townsfolk along. Have you asked the beast how to cast the spells for working the ship?"

"Yes," I answered reluctantly. "He says the rudder is very simple."

"And have you told him what will happen to him if he does not pilot us faithfully?"

"I have intimated. He says he will obey."

"Good! Then we can start in another day or two!" Sir Owain leaned back, eyes dreamily half closed. "We must eventually see about getting word back to his own people. One could buy much wine and amuse many fair women with his ransom."

Chapter III

And so we departed.

Stranger even than the ship and its advent was that embarkation. There the thing towered, like a steel cliff forged by a wizard for a hideous use. On the other side of the common huddled little Ansby, thatched cots and rutted streets, fields green beneath our wan English sky. The very castle, once so dominant in the scene, looked shrunken and gray.

But up the ramps we had let down from many levels, into the gleaming pillar, thronged our homely, red-faced, sweating, laughing people. Here John Hameward roared along with his bow across one shoulder and a tavern wench giggling on the other. There a yeoman armed with a rusty ax that might have been swung at Hastings, clad in patched wadmal, preceded a scolding wife burdened with their bedding and cooking pot, and half a dozen children clinging to her skirts. Here a crossbowman tried to make a stubborn mule climb the gangway, his oaths laying many years in Purgatory to his account. There a lad chased a pig which had gotten loose. Here a richly clad knight jested with a fine lady who bore a hooded falcon on her wrist. There a priest told his beads as he went doubtfully into the iron maw. Here a cow lowed, there a sheep bleated, here a goat shook its horns, there a hen cackled. All told, some two thousand souls went aboard.

The ship held them easily. Each important man could have a cabin for himself and his lady—for several had brought wives, lemans, or both as far as Ansby Castle, to make a more social occasion of the departure for France. The commoners spread pallets in empty holds. Poor Ansby was left almost deserted, and I often wonder if it still exists.

Sir Roger had made Branithar operate the ship on some trial flights. It had risen smoothly and silently as he worked the wheels and levers and knobs in the control turret. Steering was childishly simple, though we could make neither head nor tail of certain discs with heathenish inscriptions, across which quivered needles. Through me, Branithar told Sir Roger that the ship derived its motive power from the destruction of matter, a horrid idea indeed, and that its engines raised and propelled it by nullifying the pull of the earth along chosen directions. This was senseless— Aristotle has explained very clearly how things fall to the ground because it is their nature to fall, and I have no truck with illogical ideas to which flighty heads so easily succumb.

Despite his own reservations, the abbot joined Father Simon in blessing the ship. We named her *Crusader*. Though we only had two chaplains along, we had also borrowed a lock of St. Benedict's hair, and all who embarked had confessed and received absolution. So it was thought we were safe enough from ghostly peril, though I had my doubts.

I was given a small cabin adjoining the suite in which Sir Roger lived with his lady and their children.

Branithar was kept under guard in a near-by room. My duty was to interpret, to continue the prisoner's instruction in Latin and the education of young Robert, and to act as my lord's amanuensis.

At departure, however, the control turret was occupied by Sir Roger, Sir Owain, Branithar, and myself. It was windowless, like the entire ship, but held glassy screens in which appeared images of the earth below and all the sky around. I shivered and told my beads, for it is not lawful for Christian men to gaze into the crystal globes of Indic sorcerers.

"Now, then," said Sir Roger, and his hooked face laughed at me, "let's away! We'll be in France within the hour!"

He sat down before the panel of levers and wheels. Branithar said quickly to me: "The trial flights were only a few miles. Tell your master that for a trip of this length certain special preparations must be made."

Sir Roger nodded when I had passed this on. "Very well, let him do so." His sword slithered from the sheath. "But I'll be watching our course in the screens. At the first sign of treachery—"

Sir Owain scowled. "Is this wise, my lord?" he asked. "The beast—"

"Is our prisoner. You're too full of Celtic superstitions, Owain. Let him begin."

Branithar seated himself. The furnishings of the ship, chairs and tables and beds and cabinets, were somewhat small for us humans—and badly designed, without so much as a carven dragon for ornament. But we could make do with them. I watched the captive intently as his blue hands moved over the panel.

A deep humming trembled in the ship. I felt nothing, but the ground in the lower screens suddenly dwindled. That was sorcerous; I would much rather the usual backward thrust of a vehicle when it starts were not annulled. Fighting down my stomach, I stared into the screen-reflected vault of heaven. Erelong we were among the clouds, which proved to be high floating mists. Clearly this shows the wondrous power of God, for it is known that the angels often sit about on the clouds, and do not get wet.

"Now, southward," ordered Sir Roger.

Branithar grunted, set a dial, and snapped down a bar. I heard a clicking as of a lock. The bar stayed down.

Hellish triumph flared in the yellow eyes. Branithar sprang from his seat and snarled at me; *"Consummati estis!"* His Latin was very bad. "You are finished! I have just sent you to death!"

"What?" I cried.

Sir Roger cursed, half understanding, and lunged at the Wersgor. But the sight of what was in the screens checked him. The sword clattered from his hand, and sweat leaped out on his face.

Truly it was terrible. The earth dwindled beneath us as if it were falling down a great well. About us, the blue sky darkened, and stars glittered forth. Yet it was not nightfall, for the sun still shone in one screen, more brightly than ever!

Sir Owain screamed something in Welsh. I fell to my knees.

Branithar darted for the door. Sir Roger whirled and grasped him by his robe. They went over in a raging tangle.

Sir Owain was paralyzed by terror, and I could not pull my eyes from the horrible beauty of the spectacle about us. Earth shrank so small that it only filled one screen. It was blue, banded, with dark splotches, and round. *Round!*

A new and deeper note entered the low drone in the air. New needles on the control panel quivered to life. Suddenly we were moving, gaining speed, with impossible swiftness. An altogether different set of engines, acting on a wholly unknown principle, had unwound their ropes.

I saw the moon swell before us. Even as I stared, we passed so near that I could see mountains and pockmarks upon it, edged with their own shadows. But this was inconceivable! All knew the moon to be a perfect circle. Sobbing, I tried to break that liar of a vision screen, but could not.

Sir Roger overcame Branithar and stretched him half-conscious on the deck. The knight got up, breathing heavily. "Where are we?" he gasped. "What's happened?"

"We're going up," I groaned. "Up and out." I put my fingers in my ears so as not to be deafened when we crashed into the first of the crystal spheres.

After a while, when nothing had occurred, I opened my eyes and looked again. Earth and moon were both receding, little more than a doubled star of blue and gold. The real stars flamed hard, unwinking, against an infinite blackness. It seemed to me that we were still picking up speed.

Sir Roger cut off my prayers with an oath. "We've this traitor to handle first!" He kicked Branithar in the ribs. The Wersgor sat up and glared defiance.

I collected my wits and said to him in Latin, "What have you done? You will die by torture unless you take us back at once."

He rose, folded his arms, and regarded us with bitter pride. "Did you think that you barbarians were any match for a civilized mind?" he answered. "Do what you will with me. There will be revenge enough when you come to this journey's end."

"But what *have* you done?"

His bruised mouth grinned. "I set the ship under control of its automaton-pilot. It is now steering itself. Everything is automatic—the departure from atmosphere, the switch-over into translight quasi-velocity, the compensation for optical effects, the preservation of artificial gravity and other environmental factors."

"Well, turn off the engines!"

"No one can. I could not do so myself, now that the lock-bar is down. It will remain down until we get to Tharixan. And that is the nearest world settled by my people!"

I tried the controls, gingerly. They could not be moved. When I told the knights, Sir Owain moaned aloud.

But Sir Roger said grimly: "We'll find whether that is the truth or not. The questioning will at least punish his betrayal!"

Through me, Branithar replied with scorn: "Vent your spite if you must. I am not afraid of you. But I say that even if you broke my will, it would be useless. The rudder settings cannot be changed now, nor the ship halted. The lock-bar is meant for situations when a vessel must be sent somewhere with no one aboard." After a moment he added earnestly: "You must understand, though, I bear you no malice. You are foolhardy, but I could almost regret the fact that we need your world for ourselves. If you will spare me, I shall intercede for you when we get to Tharixan. Your own lives may be given you, at least."

Sir Roger rubbed his chin thoughtfully. I heard the bristles scratch under his palm, though he had shaved only last Thursday. "I gather the ship will become manageable again when we reach this destination," he said. I was amazed how coolly he took it after the first shock. "Could we not turn about then and go home?"

"I will never guide you!" said Branithar to that. "And alone, unable to read our navigational books, you would never find the way. We will be farther from your world than light can travel in a thousand of your years."

"You might have the courtesy not to insult our intelligence," I huffed. "I know as well as you do that light has an infinite velocity."

He shrugged.

A gleam lit Sir Roger's eye. "When will we arrive?" he asked.

"In ten days," Branithar informed us. "It is not the distances between stars, great though they are, that has made us so slow to reach your world. We have been expanding for three centuries. It is the sheer number of suns."

"Hm. When we arrive, we have this fine ship to use, with its bombards and the hand weapons. The Wersgorix may regret our visit!"

I translated for Branithar, who answered, "I sincerely advise you to surrender at once. True, these fire-beams of ours can slay a man, or reduce a city to slag. But you will find them useless, because we have screens of pure force which will stop any such beam. The ship is not so protected, since the generators of a force shield are too bulky for it. Thus the guns of the fortress can shoot upward and destroy you."

When Sir Roger heard this, he said only: "Well, we've ten days to think it over. Let this remain a secret. No one can see out of the ship, save from this place. I'll think of some tale that won't alarm the folk too much."

He went out, his cloak swirling behind him like great wings.

Chapter IV

I was the least of our troop, and much happened in which I had no part. Yet I shall set it down as fully as may be, using conjecture to fill in the gaps of knowledge. The chaplains heard much in confession, and without violating confidence they were ever quick to correct false impressions.

I believe, therefore, that Sir Roger took Catherine his lady aside and told her how matters stood. He had hoped for calm and courage from her, but she flew into the bitterest of rages.

"Ill was the day I wed you!" she cried. Her lovely face turned red and then white, and she stamped a small foot on the steel deck. "Bad enough that your oafishness should disgrace me before king and court, and doom me to yawn my life away in that bear's den you call a castle. Now you set the lives and the very souls of my children at hazard!"

"But, dearest," he stammered. "I could not know—"

"No, you were too stupid! 'Twas not enough to go

robbing and whoring off into France, you must needs
do it in this aerial coffin. Your arrogance told you the
demon was so afraid of you he would be your obedient
slave. Mary, pity women!"

She whirled, sobbing, and hurried from him.

Sir Roger stared after her till she had vanished
down the long corridor. Then, heavyhearted, he
betook himself to see his troopers.

He found them in the afterhold, cooking their sup-
per. The air remained sweet in spite of all the fires
we lit; Branithar told me the ship embodied a system
for renewing the vital spirits of the atmosphere. I
found it somewhat unnerving always to have the walls
luminous and not know day from night. But the common soldiers sat around, hoisting ale crocks, bragging,
dicing, cracking fleas, a wild, godless crew who nonetheless cheered their lord with real affection.

Sir Roger signaled to Red John Hameward, whose
huge form lumbered to join him in a small side chamber. "Well, sire," he remarked, "it seems a longish
ways to France after all."

"Plans have been, um, changed," Sir Roger told him
carefully. "It seems there may be a rare booty in the
homeland of this ship. With that, we could equip an
army large enough not only to take, but to hold and
settle all our conquests."

Red John belched and scratched under his doublet.
"If we don't run into more nor we can handle, sire."

"I think not. But you must prepare your men for
this change of plan and soothe whatever fears they
have."

"That'll not be easy, sire."

"Why not? I told you the plunder would be good."

"Well, my lord, if you want the honest truth, 'tis in
this wise. You see, though we've most of the Ansby
women along, and many of 'em are unwed and, um,
friendly disposed ... even so, my lord, the fact
remains, d' you see, we've twice as many men as

women. Now the French girls are fair, and belike the
Saracen wenches would do in a pinch—indeed, they're
said to be very pinchable—but, judging from those
blueskins we overmastered, well, their females aren't
so handsome."

"How do you know they don't hold beautiful prin-
cesses in captivity that yearn for an honest English
face?"

"That's so, my lord. It could well be."

"Then see you have the bowmen ready to fight
when we arrive." Sir Roger clapped the giant on the
shoulder and went out to speak similarly with his other
captains.

He mentioned this question of women to me somewhat later, and I was horrified. "God be praised, that
He made the Wersgorix so unattractive, if they are of
another species!" I exclaimed. "Great is His fore-
thought!"

"Ill-favored though they be," asked the baron, "are
you sure they're not human?"

"Would God I knew, sire," I answered after thinking about it. "They look like naught on earth. Yet they
do go on two legs, have hands, speech, the power of
reason."

"It matters little," he decided.

"Oh, but it matters greatly, sire!" I told him. "For
see you, if they have souls, then it is our plain duty
to win them to the Faith. But if they have not, it were
blasphemous to give them the sacraments."

"I'll let you find out which," he said indifferently.

I hurried forthwith to Branithar's cabin, which was
guarded by a couple of spearmen. "What would you?"
he asked when I sat down.

"Have you a soul?" I inquired.

"A what?"

I explained what *spiritus* meant. He was still puzzled. "Do you really think a miniature of yourself lives
in your head?" he asked.

"Oh, no. The soul is not material. It is what gives life—well, not exactly that, since animals are alive—will, the self—"

"I see. The brain."

"No, no, no! The soul is, well, that which lives on after the body is dead, and faces judgment for its actions during life."

"Ah. You believe, then, that the personality survives after death. An interesting problem. If personality is a pattern rather than a material object, as seems reasonable, then it is theoretically possible that this pattern may be transferred to something else, the same system of relationships but in another physical matrix."

"Stop maundering!" I snapped impatiently. "You are worse than an Albigensian. Tell me in plain words, do you or do you not have a soul?"

"Our scientists have investigated the problems involved in a pattern concept of personality, but, so far as I know, data are still lacking on which to base a conclusion."

"There you go again." I sighed. "Can you not give me a simple answer? Just tell me whether or not you have a soul."

"I don't know."

"You're no help at all," I scolded him, and left.

My colleagues and I debated the problem at length, but except for the obvious fact that provisional baptism could be given any nonhumans willing to receive it, no solution was reached. It was a matter for Rome, perhaps for an ecumenical council.

While all this went on, Lady Catherine had mastered her tears and swept haughtily on down a passageway, seeking to ease her inner turmoil by motion. In the long room where the captains dined, she found Sir Owain tuning his harp. He leaped to his feet and bowed. "My lady! This is a pleasant . . . I might say dazzling . . . surprise."

She sat down on a bench. "Where are we now?" she asked in sudden surrender to her weariness.

Perceiving that she knew the truth, he replied, "I don't know. Already the sun itself has shrunk till we have lost view of it among the stars." A slow smile kindled in his dark face. "Yet there is sun enough in this chamber."

Catherine felt a blush go up her cheeks. She looked down at her shoes. Her own lips stirred upward, unwilled by herself.

"We are on the loneliest voyage men ever undertook," said Sir Owain. "If my lady will permit, I'll seek to while away an hour of it with a song cycle dedicated to her charms."

She did not refuse more than once. His voice rose until it filled the room.

Chapter V

There is a little to tell of the outward journey. The tedium of it soon bulked larger than the perils. Knights exchanged harsh words, and John Hameward had to crack more than one pair of heads together to keep order among his bowmen. The serfs took it best; when not caring for livestock, or eating, they merely slept.

I noticed that Lady Catherine was often at converse with Sir Owain, and that her husband was no longer overjoyed about it. However, he was always caught up in some plan or preparation, and the younger knight did give her hours of distraction, even of merriment.

Sir Roger and I spent much time with Branithar, who was willing enough to tell us about his race and its empire. I was reluctantly coming to believe his claims. Strange that so ugly a breed should dwell in what I judged to be the Third Heaven, but the fact could not be denied. Belike, I thought, when Scripture mentioned the four corners of the world, it did not mean our planet Terra at all, but referred to a cubical universe. Beyond this must lie the abode of the blessed; while Branithar's remark about the molten interior of the earth was certainly consonant with prophetic visions of hell.

Branithar told us that there were about a hundred worlds like our own in the Wersgor empire. They circled as many separate stars, for no sun was likely to have more than one habitable planet. Each of these worlds was the dwelling place of a few million Wersgorix, who liked plenty of room. Except for the capital planet, Wersgorixan, they bore no cities. But those on the frontiers of the empire, like Tharixan whither we were bound, had fortresses which were also space-navy bases. Branithar stressed the firepower and impregnability of these castles.

If a usable planet had intelligent natives, these were either exterminated or enslaved. The Wersgorix did no menial work, leaving this to such helots, or to automata. Themselves they were soldiers, managers of their vast estates, traders, owners of manufactories, politicians, and courtiers. Being unarmed, the enslaved natives had no hope of revolting against the relatively small number of alien masters. Sir Roger muttered something about distributing weapons to these oppressed beings when we arrived and telling them about the Jacquerie. But Branithar guessed his intent, laughed, and said Tharixan had never been inhabited, so there were only a few hundred slaves on the entire planet.

This empire filled a rough sphere in space, about two thousand light-years across. (A light-year being the incredible distance that light covers in one standard Wersgor year, which Branithar said was about 10 percent longer than the Terrestrial period.) It included millions of suns with their worlds. But most of these, because of poisonous air or poisonous life forms or other things, were useless to the Wersgorix and ignored.

Sir Roger asked if they were the only nation which had learned to fly between the stars. Branithar shrugged contemptuously. "We have encountered three others, who developed the art independently," he said. "They live within the sphere of our empire, but so far we have not subdued them. It was not worth while, when primitive planets are such easier game. We allow these three races to traffic, and to keep the small number of colonies they had already established in other planetary systems. But we have not allowed them to continue expanding. A couple of minor wars settled that. They have no love for us: they know we will destroy them someday when it is convenient for us to do so, but they are helpless in the face of overwhelming power."

"I see," nodded the baron.

He instructed me to start learning the Wersgor language. Branithar found it amusing to teach me, and I could smother my own fears by hard work, so it went quite fast. Their tongue was barbarous, lacking the noble inflections of Latin, but on that account not hard to master.

In the control turret I found drawers full of charts and numerical tables. All the writing was beautifully exact; I thought they must have such scribes it was a pity they had not gone on to illuminate the pages. Puzzling over these, and using what I had learned of the Wersgor speech and alphabet, I decided this was a set of navigational directions.

A regular map of the planet Tharixan was included, since this had been the home base of the expedition. I translated the symbols for land, sea, river, fortress, and so on. Sir Roger pored long hours over it. Even the Saracen chart his grandfather had brought back from the Holy Land was crude compared to this; though on the other hand the Wersgorix showed lack of culture by omitting pictures of mermaids, the four winds, hippogriffs, and similar ornamentation.

I also deciphered the legends on some of the control panel instruments. Such dials as those for altitude and speed could readily be mastered. But what did "fuel flow" mean? What was the difference between "sublight drive" and "super-light drive"? Truly these were potent, though pagan, charms.

And so the sameness of days passed, and after a time which felt like a century we observed that one star was waxing in the screens. It swelled until it flamed big and bright as our own sun. And then we saw a planet, similar to ours save that it had two small moons. Downward we plunged, till the scene was not a ball in the sky but a great rugged sweep of landscape under our footsoles. When I saw heaven again turned blue, I threw myself to the deck in thanksgiving.

The lock-bar snapped upward. The ship came to a halt and hung where it was, a mile in the air. We had reached Tharixan.

Chapter VI

Sir Roger had summoned me to the control turret, with Sir Owain and Red John, who led Branithar on a leash. The bowman gaped at the screens and muttered horrid oaths.

Word had gone through the ship that all fighting men must arm themselves. The two knights here were in plate, their esquires waiting outside with shields and helmets. Horses stamped in the holds and along the corridors. Women and children huddled back with bright fearful eyes.

"Here we are!" Sir Roger grinned. It was eldritch to see him so boyishly gay, when everyone else was swallowing hard and sweating till the air reeked. But a fight, even against the powers of hell, was something he could understand. "Brother Parvus, ask the prisoner where we are on the planet."

I put the question to Branithar, who touched a control button. A hitherto blank screen glowed to life, showing a map. "We are where the cross hairs center," he told us. "The map will unroll as we fly about."

I compared the screen with the chart in my hand. "The fortress called Ganturath seems to lie about a hundred miles north by northeast, my lord," I said.

Branithar, who had been picking up a little English, nodded. "Ganturath is only a minor base." He must put his boasts into Latin still. "Yet numerous space-ships are stationed there, and swarms of aircraft. The fire-weapons on the ground can blast this vessel out of existence, and force screens will stop any beams from your own guns. Best you surrender."

When I had translated, Sir Owain said slowly: "It may be the wisest thing, my lord."

"What?" cried Sir Roger. "An Englishman yield without a fight?"

"But the women, sire, and the poor little children!"

"I am not a rich man," said Sir Roger. "I cannot afford to pay ransom." He clumped in his armor to the pilot's chair, sat down, and tapped the manual controls.

Through the downward vision screens, I saw the land slide swiftly away beneath us. Its rivers and mountains were of homelike shape, but the vegetation's green hues were overlaid with a weird bluish tint. The country seemed wild. Now and again we saw a few rounded buildings, amidst enormous grainfields cultivated by machines, but otherwise it was bare of man as the New Forest. I wondered if this, too, were some king's hunting preserve, then remembered Branithar's account of sparse habitation everywhere in the Wersgor Empire.

A voice broke our silence, chattering away in the harsh blue-face language. We started, crossed ourselves, and glared about. The sounds came from a small black instrument affixed to the main panel.

"So!" Red John drew his dagger. "All this time

there's been a stowaway! Give me a crowbar, sire, and I'll pry him out."

Branithar divined his meaning. Laughter barked in the thick blue throat. "The voice is borne from afar, by waves like those of light but longer," he said.

"Talk sense!" I demanded.

"Well, we are being hailed by an observer at Ganturath fortress."

Sir Roger nodded curtly when I translated. "Voices out of thin air are little compared to what we've already seen," he said. "What does the fellow want?"

I could catch only a few words of the challenge, but got the drift of it. Who were we? This was not the regular landing place for scout craft. Why did we enter a forbidden area? "Calm them," I instructed Branithar, "and remember I will understand if you betray us."

He shrugged, as if amused, though his own brow was also filmed with sweat. "Scoutship 587-*Zin* returning," he said. "Urgent message. Will halt above the base."

The voice gave assent, but warned that if we came lower than a *stanthax* (about half a mile), we would be destroyed. We were to hover until the crews of patrol aircraft could board us.

By now, Ganturath was visible: a compact mass of domes and half-cylinders, masonry over steel skeletons as we later found out. It made a circle about a thousand feet in diameter. Half a mile or so northward lay a smaller set of buildings. Through a magnifying view screen, we saw that out of the latter jutted the muzzles of huge fire-bombards.

Even as we came to a halt, a pale shimmering sprang up around both parts of the fortress. Branithar pointed. "The defensive screens. Your own shots would spatter harmlessly off. It would be a lucky hit that melted one of those gun muzzles, where they thrust out beyond the shield. But you are an easy target."

Several egg-shaped metallic craft, like midges against the huge bulk of our *Crusader,* approached. We saw others lift from the ground, the main part of the fortress. Sir Roger's fair head nodded. " 'Tis as I thought," he said. "Those screens stop a fire-beam, mayhap, but not a material object, since the boats pass through."

"True," said Branithar by way of me. "You might manage to drop an explosive missile or two, but the outlying section, where the guns are, would destroy you."

"Aha." Sir Roger studied the Wersgor with eyes gone pale. "So you possess explosive shells, eh? Doubtless aboard this very craft. And you never told me. We'll see about that later." He jerked a thumb at Red John and Sir Owain. "Well, you two have seen how the ground lies. Go back to the men, now, and be ready to emerge fighting when we land."

They departed, nervously eyeing the screens, where the aircraft were very near us. Sir Roger put his own hands on the wheels that controlled the bombards. We had learned, with some experimentation, that those great weapons almost aimed and fired themselves. As the patrol boats closed in, Sir Roger cut loose.

Blinding hell-beams stabbed forth. They wrapped the aircraft in flame. I saw the nearest one cut in two by that fiery sword. Another tumbled red-hot, a third exploded. Thunder boomed. Then all I saw was falling metal scrap.

Sir Roger tested Branithar's claims, but they were true: his beams splashed off that pale, translucent screen. He grunted. "I looked for that. Best we get down now before they send up a real warship to deal with us, or open fire from the outlying emplacement." While he spoke, he sent us hurtling groundward. A flame touched our hull, but then we were too low. I saw Ganturath's buildings rush up to meet me and braced myself for death.

A ripping and crunching went through our ship. This very turret burst open as it brushed a low lookout tower. But the battlements of that were snapped off. Two thousand feet long, incalculably heavy, the *Crusader* squashed half Ganturath beneath itself.

Sir Roger was on his feet even before the engines went dead. "Haro!" he bellowed. "God send the right!" And off he went, across the canted, buckled deck. He snatched his helmet from the terrified esquire and put it on as he strode. The boy followed, teeth chattering but nonetheless in charge of the de Tourneville shield.

Branithar sat speechless. I gathered up my robe and hurried off to find a sergeant who would lock up the valuable captive for me. This being done, I was able to witness the battle.

We had come down lengthwise rather than on our tail, protected by the artificial weight generators from tumbling around inside. Havoc encompassed us, smashed buildings and sharded walls. A chaos of blue Wersgorix boiled from the rest of the fortress.

By the time I got to the exit myself, Sir Roger was out with all his cavalry. He didn't stop to gather them, but charged into the thick of the nearest enemies. His horse neighed, mane flying, armor flashing; the long lance spitted three bodies at once. When at length the spear was broken, my lord drew his sword and hewed lustily. Most of his followers had no scruples about unknightly weapons; they eked out blade, mace, and morningstar with handguns from the ship.

Now archers and men-at-arms poured forth, yelling. Belike it was their own terror that made them so savage. They closed with the Wersgonix ere our foe could unleash many lightning bolts. The battle became hand-to-hand, a leaderless riot, where ax or dagger or quarterstaff was more useful than fire-beam or pellet gun.

When the space about him was cleared, Sir Roger reared on his black stallion. He clashed back his visor and set bugle to lips. It shrieked through the din, summoning the mounted force. These, better disciplined than the foot soldiers, disengaged themselves from the immediate fray and joined the baron. A mass of great horses, men like steel towers, blazoned shields and flying plumes and lances aloft, formed behind my lord.

His gauntleted hand pointed to the outlying fort, where the skyward bombards had ceased their futile shooting. "That we must seize, ere they rally!" he cried. "After me, Englishmen, for God and St. George!"

He took a fresh shaft from his esquire, spurred his charger, and began to pick up speed. The earthquake roll of hoofs deepened behind him.

Those Wersgorix stationed in the lesser fort poured out to resist the attack. They had guns of several kinds, plus small explosive missiles to be thrown by hand. They picked off a couple of riders. But in that short distance there was no time for more long-range shooting. And they were unnerved in any event. There is no sight more terrifying than a charge of heavy cavalry.

The trouble of the Wersgorix was that they had gone too far. They had made combat on the ground obsolete, and were ill-trained, ill-equipped, when it happened. True, they possessed fire-beams, as well as force shields to stop those same fire-beams. But they had never thought to lay down caltrops.

As it was, the frightful blow struck their line, rolled over it, stamped it into mud, and continued without even being slowed.

One of the buildings beyond gaped open. A small spaceship—though big as any seagoing vessel on Earth—had been trundled forth. It stood on its tail, engine growling, ready to take off and flame us from above. Sir Roger directed his cavalry thither. The lancers hit it in a single line. Shafts splintered; men were hurled from the saddle. But consider: a charging cavalryman may bear his own weight of armor, and have fifteen hundred pounds of horse beneath him. The whole travels at several miles per hour. The impact is awesome.

The ship was bowled over. It fell on its side and lay crippled.

Through and through the lesser fort, Sir Roger's horsemen ramped, sword, mace, spurred boot, and shod hoof. The Wersgorix died like swatted flies. Or say rather, the flies were the small patrol boats, buzzing overhead, unable to shoot into that melee without killing their own folk. To be sure, Sir Roger was killing their own folk anyway; but by the time the Wersgorix realized that, they were too late.

Back in the main section where the *Crusader* lay, the fight sputtered down into a question of slaying bluefaces or taking them prisoner or chasing them into the near-by forest. It was still one vast confusion, though, and Red John Hameward felt he was wasting the skill of his longbowmen. He formed them into a detachment and quick-stepped across open ground to aid Sir Roger.

The patrol boats swooped low, hungrily. Here was prey they might get. Their thin beams were intended for short ranges. On the first pass, two archers died. Then Red John yelled an order.

Suddenly the sky was full of arrows. A cloth-yard shaft with a six-foot yew bow behind it will go through an armored man and the horse beneath him. These little boats made matters worse by flying directly into the gray goose flock. Not one of them escaped. Riddled, their pilots quilled as hedgehogs, they crashed. The archers roared and ran to join the fray ahead.

The spaceship which the lancers had knocked over

was still manned. Its crew must have recovered their wits. Suddenly its gun turrets spurted flame, no mere handweapon beam but thunderbolts that knocked down walls. A horseman and his steed, caught in that fire, were instantly gone. Vengefully, the lightnings raked around.

Red John picked up one end of a great steel beam, part of the dome shattered by those bombards. Fifty men aided him. They ran toward the entry port of the ship. Once, twice, crash! Down came the door, and the English yeomen stormed within.

The Battle of Ganturath lasted for some hours, but most of that time went merely to ferret out hidden remnants of the garrison. When the alien sun smoldered westward, there were about a score of English dead. None were badly wounded, for the flame guns usually killed if they hit the mark at all. Some three hundred Wersgorix were slain, roughly an equal number captured; many of these latter were minus a limb or an ear. I would guess that perhaps a hundred more escaped on foot. They would carry word of us to the nearest estates—which, however, were not very close by. Evidently the speed and destructiveness of our initial attack had put Ganturath's far-speakers out of action before the alarm could go abroad.

Our true disaster was not revealed till later. We were not dismayed at having wrecked the ship we came in, for we now had several other vessels whose aggregate volume would hold us all. Their crews had never gotten a chance to man them. However, in her atrocious landing, the *Crusader* had burst open her control turret. And the Wersgor navigational notes therein were now lost.

At the moment, all was triumph. Red-splashed, panting, in scorched and dinted armor, Sir Roger de Tourneville rode a weary horse back to the main fortress. After him came the lancers, archers, yeomen— ragged, battered, shoulders slumped with exhaustion.

But the Te Deum was on their lips, rising beneath the strange constellations that twinkled forth, and their banners flew bravely against the sky.

It was wonderful to be an Englishman.

Chapter VII

We made camp at the nearly intact lesser fort. Our people chopped wood from the forest, and as the two moons rose, their blazes leaped up. Men sat close, faces picked out of darkness by the homely unrestful light, waiting for the stewpots to be ready. Horses cropped the native grass without enjoying its taste. The captured Wersgorix huddled together under guard of pikemen. They were stunned; this did not seem possible. I felt almost sorry for them, godless and cruel though their dominion was.

Sir Roger summoned me to join his captains, who were camped near one of the gun turrets. We manned what defenses were available, against expected counterattack, and tried not to wonder what new frightfulness the foe might have in their armory.

Tents had been erected for the more wellborn ladies. Most were abed, but Lady Catherine sat on a stool at the edge of the firelight. She listened to our talk, and her mouth was drawn into bleak lines.

The captains sprawled, weary, on the ground. I saw Sir Owain Montbelle, idly thrumming his harp; scarred, fierce old Sir Brian Fitz-William, the third of the three knighted men on this voyage; big Alfred Edgarson, the purest of Saxon franklins; gloomy Thomas Bullard, fingering the naked sword on his lap; Red John Hameward, shy because he was the lowest born of them all. A couple of pages poured wine.

My lord Sir Roger, the unbendable, was on his feet, hands clasped behind his back. Having removed his armor like the others, while leaving his clothes of pride in their chest, he might have been the humblest of his own sergeants. But then one saw the sinewy jut-nosed face and heard him talk. And spurs jingled on his boots.

He nodded as I came into view. "Ah, there, Brother Parvus. Sit down and have a stoup. You've a head on your chine, and we need all good redes tonight."

A while longer he paced, brooding. I dared not interrupt with my dreadful news. A medley of noises in the dark deepened its twin-mooned otherness. These were not frogs and crickets and nightjars of England: here was a buzz, a saw-toothed hum, an inhumanly sweet singing like a lute of steel. And the odors were alien, too, which disturbed me even more.

"Well," said my lord. "By God's grace, we've won this first encounter. Now we must decide what to do next."

"I think—" Sir Owain cleared his throat, then spoke hurriedly: "No, gentles, I am sure. God aided us against unforeseeable treachery. He will not be with us if we show undue pride. We've won a rare booty of weapons, with which we can accomplish great things at home. Let us therefore start back at once."

Sir Roger tugged his chin. "I'd liefer stay here," he answered, "yet there's much in what you say, my friend. We can always come back, after the Holy Land is freed, and do a proper job on this fiend's nest."

"Aye," nodded Sir Brian. "We're too alone now, and encumbered with women and children and aged and livestock. So few fighting men against a whole empire, that were madness."

"Yet I could like to break another spear against these Wersgorix," said Alfred Edgarson. "I haven't won any gold here yet."

"Gold is no use unless we bring it home," Captain Bullard reminded him. "Bad enough campaigning in the heat and thirst of the Holy Land. Here, we know not even what plants may be poisonous, or what the winter season is like. Best we depart tomorrow."

A rumble of assent went up among them.

I cleared my throat miserably. Branithar and I had just spent a most unpleasant hour. "My lords—" I began.

"Yes? What is it?" Sir Roger glared at me.

"My lords, I do not think we can find the way home!"

"What?" They roared it out. Several leaped to their feet. I heard Lady Catherine suck a horrified breath in between her teeth.

Then I explained that the Wersgor notes on the route to our sun were missing from the shattered control turret. I had led a search party, scratching about everywhere in the attempt to find them, but had no success. The interior of the turret was blackened, melted in places. I could only conclude that a stray fire-beam had come through the hole, played across a drawer burst open by the violence of our landing, and cindered the papers.

"But Branithar knows the way!" protested Red John. "He sailed it himself! I'll wring it out of him, my lord."

"Be not so hasty," I counseled. " 'Tis not like sailing along a coastline, where every landmark is known. There are uncounted millions of stars. This scouting expedition zigzagged among them looking for a suitable planet. Without figures which the captain wrote down as they sailed, one might spend a lifetime in search and not happen on our own sun."

"But doesn't Branithar remember?" yelped Sir Owain.

"Remember a hundred pages of numbers?" I responded. "Nay, none could do that, and this is the more true since Branithar was not the captain of the ship nor the one who kept track of her wanderings and heaved the log and performed other navigational duties, rather our captive was a lesser noble whose task was more among the crewmen and in working with the demonic engines than—"

"Enough." Sir Roger gnawed his lip and stared at the ground. "This changes things. Yes. . . . Was not the *Crusader*'s route known in advance? Say by the duke who sent her out?"

"No, my lord," I said. "Wersgor scoutships merely go off in any direction the captain likes and look at any star he deems promising. Not till they come back and report does their duke know where they have been."

A groan went up. Those were hardy men, but this was enough to daunt the Nine Worthies. Sir Roger walked stiffly over to his wife and laid a hand on her arm.

"I'm sorry, my dear," he mumbled.

She turned her face from him.

Sir Owain arose. The knuckles stood forth pale on the hand that clutched his harp. "This have you led us to!" he shrilled. "To death and damnation beyond the sky! Are you satisfied?"

Sir Roger clapped hand on hilt. "Be still!" he roared. "All of you agreed with my plan. Not a one of you demurred. None were forced to come. We must all share the burden now, or God pity us!"

The younger knight muttered rebelliously but sat down again.

It was awesome how swiftly my lord rebounded

from dismay to boldness. Of course it was a mask he put on for the others' benefit; but how many men could have done that much? Truly he was a peerless leader. I attribute it to the blood of King William the Conqueror, a bastard grandson of whom wed an illegitimate daughter of that Earl Godfrey who was later outlawed for piracy, and so founded the noble de Tourneville house.

"Come, now," said the baron with a degree of cheerfulness. " 'Tis not so bad. We've but to act with steadfast hearts, and the day shall yet be ours. Remember, we hold a good number of captives, whom we can use as a bargaining point. If we must fight again, we've already proven they cannot withstand us under anything like equal conditions. I admit there are more of them, and that they have more skill with these craven hell-weapons. But what of that? 'Twill not be the first time brave men properly led have driven a seemingly stronger army from the field."

"At the very worst, we can retreat. We have sky-ships enough, and can evade pursuit in the trackless deeps of space. But I'm fain to stay here, bargain shrewdly, fight where needful, and put my trust in God. Surely He, who stopped the sun for Joshua, can swat a million Wersgorix if it pleases Him: for His mercy endureth forever. After we've wrung terms from the foe, we'll make them find our home for us and stuff our ships with gold. I say to you, hold fast! For the glory of God, the honor of England, and the enrichment of us all!"

He caught them up, bore them on the wave of his own spirit, and had them cheering him at the end. They crowded close, hands on his hands above his great shining sword, and swore to remain true till the danger was past. Thereafter an hour went in eager planning—most of it, alas, wasted, for God seldom brings that to pass which man expects. Finally all went to their rest.

I saw my lord take his wife's arm to lead her into his pavilion. She spoke to him, a harsh whisper, she would not hear his protests but stood there denouncing him in the enemy night. The larger moon, already sinking, touched them with cold fire.

Sir Roger's shoulders slumped. He turned and went slowly from her, wrapped himself in a saddle blanket, and slept in the dews of the field.

It was strange that a man among men was so helpless against a woman. He had something beaten and pitiful about him as he lay there. I thought it boded ill for us.

Chapter VIII

We had been too excited at first to pay attention, and afterward we slept too long. But when I woke again, finding it still dark, I checked the movement of stars against trees. Ah, how slowly! The night here was many times as long as on Earth.

This unnerved our folk badly enough in itself. The fact that we did not flee (by now, it could no longer be concealed that treason, rather than desire, had brought us hither) puzzled many. But at least they expected weeks to carry out whatever the baron decided.

The shock, when enemy ships appeared even before dawn, was great.

"Be of good heart," I counseled Red John, as he shivered with his bowman in the gray mists. " 'Tis not that they have powers magical. You were warned of this at the captains' council. 'Tis only that they can talk across hundreds of miles and fly such distances in minutes. So as soon as one of the fugitives reached another estate, the word of us went abroad."

"Well," said Red John, not unreasonably, "if that's not magic, I'd like to know what is."

"If magic, you need have no fear," I answered, "for the black arts do not prevail against good Christian men. However, I tell you again, this is mere skill in the mechanic and warlike arts."

"And those do prevail against g-g-good Christian men!" blubbered an archer. John cuffed him to silence, while I cursed my own clumsy tongue.

In that wan, tricky light, we could see many ships hovering, some of them as big as our broken *Crusader*. My knees drummed under my cassock. Of course, we were all inside the force screen of the smaller fort, which had never been turned off. Our gunners had already discovered that the fire-bombards placed here had controls as simple as any in the spaceship, and stood prepared to shoot. However, I knew we had no true defense. One of those very powerful explosive shells whereof I had heard hints could be fired. Or the Wersgorix might attack on foot, overwhelming us with sheer numbers.

Yet those ships did only hover, in utter silence under the unknown stars. When at length the first pale dawnlight streamed off their flanks, I left the bowmen and fumbled through dew-wet grass to the cavalry. Sir Roger sat peering heavenward from his saddle. He was armed cap-a-pie, helmet in the crook of an arm, and none could tell from his face how little sleep had been granted him.

"Good morning, Brother Parvus," he said. "That was a long darkness."

Sir Owain, mounted close by, wet his lips. He was pale, his large long-lashed eyes sunken in dark rims. "No midwinter night in England ever wore away so slowly," he said, and crossed himself.

"The more daylight, then," said Sir Roger. He seemed almost cheerful, now when he dealt with foemen rather than unruly womenfolk.

Sir Owain's voice cracked across like a dry twig. "Why don't they attack?" he yelled, "Why do they just wait up there?"

"It should be obvious. I never thought 'twould need mentioning," said Sir Roger. "Have they not good reason to be afraid of us?"

"What?" I said. "Well, sire, of course we *are* Englishmen. However—" My glance traveled back, over the pitiful few tents pitched around the fortress walls; over ragged, sooty soldiers; over huddled women and grandsires, wailing children; over cattle, pigs, sheep, fowl, tended by cursing serfs; over pots where breakfast porridge bubbled—"However, my lord," I finished, "at the moment we look more French."

The baron grinned. "What do they know about French and English? For that matter, my father was at Bannockburn, where a handful of tattered Scottish pikemen broke the chivalry of King Edward II. Now all the Wersgorix know about us is that we have suddenly come from nowhere and—if Branithar's boasts be true—done what no other host has ever achieved: taken one of their strongholds! Would you not move warily, were you their constable?"

The guffaw that went up among the horse troopers spread down to the foot, until our whole camp rocked with it. I saw how the enemy prisoners shuddered and shrank close together when that wolfish noise smote them.

As the sun rose, a few Wersgor boats landed very slowly and carefully, a mile or so away. We held our fire, so they took heart and sent out people who began to erect machinery on the field.

"Are you going to let them build a castle under our very noses?" cried Thomas Bullard.

" 'Tis less likely they'll attack us, if they feel a little more secure," the baron answered. "I want it made plain that we'll parley." His smile turned wry. "Remember, friends, our best weapon now is our tongues."

Soon the Wersgorix landed many ships in a circular formation—like those stonehenges which giants raised in England before the Flood—to form a camp walled by the eerie faint shimmer of a force screen, picketed by mobile bombards, and roofed by hovering warcraft. Only when this was done did they send a herald.

The squat shape strode boldly enough across the meadows, though well aware that we could shoot him down. His metallic garments were dazzling in the morning sun, but we discerned his empty hands held open. Sir Roger himself rode forth, accompanied by myself gulping Our Fathers on a palfrey.

The Wersgor shied a trifle, as the huge black stallion and the iron tower astride it loomed above him. Then he gathered a shaky breath and said, "If you behave yourselves, I will not destroy you for the space of this discussion."

Sir Roger laughed when I had fumblingly translated. "Tell him," he ordered me, "that I in turn will hold my private lightnings in check, though they are so powerful I can't swear they may not trickle forth and blast his camp to ruin if he moves too swiftly."

"But you haven't any such lightnings at your command, sire," I protested. "It wouldn't be honest to claim you do."

"You will render my words faithfully and with a straight face, Brother Parvus," he said, "or discover something about thunderbolts."

I obeyed. In what follows I shall as usual make no note of the difficulties of translation. My Wersgor vocabulary was limited, and I daresay my grammar was ludicrous. In all events, I was only the parchment on which these puissant ones wrote, erased, and wrote again. Aye, in truth I felt like a palimpsest ere that hour was done.

Oh, the things I was forced to say! Above all men do I reverence that valiant and gentle knight Sir Roger de Tourneville. Yet when he blandly spoke of his

English estate—the small one, which only took up three planets—and of his personal defense of Roncesvaux against four million paynim, and his singlehanded capture of Constantinople on a wager, and the time guesting in France when he accepted his host's invitation to exercise the *droit de seigneur* for two hundred peasant weddings on the same day—and more and more—his words nigh choked me, though I am accounted well versed both in courtly romances and the lives of the saints. My sole consolation was that little of this shameless mendacity got through the language difficulties, the Wersgor herald understanding merely (after a few attempts to impress us) that here was a person who could outbluster him any day of the week.

Therefore he agreed on behalf of his lord that there would be a truce while matters were discussed in a shelter to be erected midway between the two camps. Each side might send a score of people thither at high noon, unarmed. While the truce lasted, no ships were to be flown within sight of either camp.

"So!" exclaimed Sir Roger gaily, as we cantered back. "I've not done so ill, have I?"

"K-k-k-k," I answered. He slowed to a smoother pace, and I tried again: "Indeed, sire, St. George—or more likely, I fear, St. Dismas, patron of thieves—must have watched over you. And yet—"

"Yes?" he prompted me. "Be not afraid to speak your mind, Brother Parvus." With a kindness wholly unmerited: "Ofttimes I think you've more head on those skinny shoulders than all my captains lumped together."

"Well, my lord," I blurted, "you've wrung concessions from them for a while. As you foretold, they are being cautious whilst they study us. And yet, how long can we hope to fool them? They have been an imperial race for centuries. They must have experience of many strange peoples living under many different conditions. From our small numbers, our antiquated weapons, our lack of home-built spaceships, will they not soon deduce the truth and attack us with overwhelming force?"

His lips thinned. He looked toward the pavilion which housed his lady and children.

"Of course," he said. "I hope but to stay their hand a short while."

"And what then?" I pursued him.

"I don't know." Whirling on me, fierce as a stooping hawk, he added: "But 'tis my secret, d' you understand? I tell it to you as if in confession. Let it come out, let our folk know how troubled and planless I truly am . . . and we're all done."

I nodded. Sir Roger struck spurs to his horse and galloped into camp, shouting like a boy.

Chapter IX

During the long wait before Tharixan reached its noontide, my master summoned his captains to a council. A trestle table was erected before the central building, and there we all sat.

"By God's grace," he said, "we're spared awhile. You'll note that I've even made them land all their ships. I'll wrangle to win us as much more respite as may be. That time must be put to use. We must strengthen our defenses. Also, we'll ransack this fort, seeking especially maps, books, and other sources of information. Those of our men who're at all gifted in the mechanic arts must study and test every machine we find, so that we can learn how to erect force screens and fly and otherwise match our foes. But all this has to be done secretly, in places hidden from enemy eyes. For if ever they learn we don't already know all about such implements—" He smiled and drew a finger across his throat.

Good Father Simon, his chaplain, turned a little green. "Must you?" he said faintly.

Sir Roger nodded at him. "I've work for you, too. I shall need Brother Parvus to interpret Wersgor for me. But we have one prisoner, Branithar, who speaks Latin—"

"I would not say that, sire," I interrupted. "His declensions are atrocious, and what he does to irregular verbs may not be described in gentle company."

"Nevertheless, until he's mastered enough English, a cleric is needed to talk to him. You see, he must explain whatever our students of the captured engines do not understand, and must interpret for any other Wersgor prisoners whom we may question."

"Ah, but will he do so?" said Father Simon. "He is a most recalcitrant heathen, my son, if indeed he has any soul at all. Why, only a few days ago on the ship, in hopes of softening his hard heart, I stood in his cell reading aloud the generations from Adam to Noah, and had scarcely gotten past Jared when I saw that he had fallen asleep!"

"Have him brought hither," commanded my lord. "Also, find One-Eyed Hubert and tell him to come in full regalia."

While we waited, talking in hushed voices, Alfred Edgarson noticed how I sat quiet. "Well, now, Brother Parvus," he boomed, "what ails you? Methinks you've little to fear, being a godly fellow. Even the rest of us, if we conduct ourselves well, have naught to fear but a sweating time in Purgatory. And then we'll join St. Michael at sentry-go on heaven's walls. Not so?"

I was loath to dishearten them by voicing what had occurred to me, but when they insisted, I said, "Alas, good men, worse may already have befallen us."

"Well?" barked Sir Brian Fitz-William. "What is it? Don't just sit there sniveling!"

"We had no sure way to tell time on the voyage hither," I whispered. "Hourglasses are too inaccurate, and since reaching this devil-made place we've neglected even to turn them. How long is the day here? What time is it on our earth?"

Sir Brian looked a trifle blank. "Indeed, I know not. What of it?"

"I presume you had a haunch of beef to break your fast," I said. "Are you sure it is not Friday?"

They gasped and regarded each other with round eyes.

"When is it Sunday?" I cried. "Will you tell me the date of Advent? How shall we observe Lent and Easter, with two moons morris-dancing about to confuse the issue?"

Thomas Bullard buried his face in his hands. "We're ruined!"

Sir Roger stood up. "No!" he shouted into the strickenness. "I'm no priest, nor even very godly. But did not Our Lord himself say the Sabbath was made for man and not man for the Sabbath?"

Father Simon looked doubtful. "I can grant special dispensations under extraordinary circumstances," he said, "but I am really not sure how far I can strain such powers."

"I like it not," mumbled Bullard. "I take this to be a sign that God has turned His face from us, withdrawing the due times of the fasts and sacraments."

Sir Roger grew red. He stood a moment more, watching the courage drain from his men like wine from a broken cup. Then he calmed himself, laughed aloud, and cried:

"Did not Our Lord command His followers to go forth as far as they were able, bringing His word, and He would be with them always? But let's not bandy texts. Perhaps we are venially sinning in this matter. Well, if that be so, a man should not grovel but should make amends. We'll make costly offerings in atonement. To get the means for such offerings . . . have we not the entire Wersgor Empire to hand, to squeeze for a ransom till its yellow eyes pop? This proves that

God Himself has commanded us to this war!" He drew his sword, blinding in the daylight, and held it before him hilt uppermost. "By this, my knightly sigil and arm, which is also the sign of the Cross, I vow to do battle for God's glory!"

He tossed the weapon so it swung glittering in the hot air, caught it again and swung it so it shrieked. "With this blade will I fight!"

The men gave him a rather feeble cheer. Only glum Bullard hung back. Sir Roger leaned down to that captain, and I heard him hiss: "The clinching proof of my reasoning is, that I'll cut anyone who argues further into dogmeat."

Actually, I felt that in his crude way my master had gasped truth. In my spare time I would recast his logic into proper syllogistic form, to make sure; but meanwhile I was much encouraged, and the others were at least not demoralized.

Now a man-at-arms fetched Branithar, who stood glaring at us. "Good day," said Sir Roger mildly, through me. "We shall want you to help interrogate prisoners and instruct us in our studies of captured engines."

The Wersgor drew himself up with a warrior's pride. "Save your breath," he spat. "Behead me and be done with it. I misjudged your capabilities once, and it has cost many lives of my people. I shall not betray them further."

Sir Roger nodded. "I looked for such an answer," he said. "What became of One-Eyed Hubert?"

"Here I am, sire, here I am, here's good old Hubert," and the baron's executioner hobbled up, adjusting his hood. The ax was tucked under one scrawny arm, and the noosed rope laid around his hump. "I was only wandering about, sire, picking flowers for me youngest granchild, sire. You know her, the little girl with long gold curls and she's so honey-sweet fond o' daisies. I hoped I could find one or other o' these paynim blooms might remind her o' our dear Lincolnshire daisies, and we could weave a daisy chain together—"

"I've work for you," said Sir Roger.

"Ah, yes, sire, yes, yes, indeed." The old man's single rheumy eye blinked about, he rubbed his hands and chuckled. "Ah, thank you, sire! 'Tis not that I mean to criticize, that ain't old Hubert's place, and he knows his humble place, him who has served man and boy, and his father and grandsire afore him, executioners to the noble de Tournevilles. No, sire, I knows me place and I keeps it as Holy Writ commands. But God's truth, you've kept poor old Hubert very idle all these years. Now your father, sire, Sir Raymond, him we called Raymond Red-Hand, there was a man what appreciated art! Though I remember his father, your grandsire, me lord, old Nevil Rip-Talon, and his justice was the talk o' three shires. In his day, sire, the commons knew their place and gentlefolk could get a decent servant at a decent wage, not like now when you let 'em off with a fine or maybe a day in the stocks. Why, 'tis a scandal—"

"Enough," said Sir Roger. "The blueface here is stubborn. Can you persuade him?"

"Well, sire! Well, well, well!" Hubert sucked toothless gums with a pure and simple delight. He walked around our rigid captive, studying him from all angles, "Well, sire, now this is another matter, 'tis like the good old days come back, 'tis, yes, yes, yes, Heaven bless my good kind master! Now o' course I took little equipment with me, only a few thumbscrews and pincers and suchlike, but it won't take me no time, sire, to knock together a rack. And maybe we can get a nice kettle of oil. I always says, sire, on a cold gray day there ain't nothing so cozy as a glowing brazier and a nice hot kettle of oil. I think o' my dear old daddy and I gets tears in this old eye, yes, sire, that

I do. Let me see, let me see, tum-te-tum-te-tum." He began measuring Branithar with his rope.

The Wersgor flinched away. His smattering of English was enough to give him the drift of conversation. "You won't!" he yelled. "No civilized folk would ever—"

"Now let's just see your hand, if you please." Hubert took a thumbscrew from his pouch and held it against the blue fingers. "Yes, yes, 'twill fit snug and proper." He unpacked an array of little knives. *"Sumer is icumen in,"* he hummed, *"lhude sing cucu."*

Branithar gulped. "But you're not civilized," he said weakly. Choking and snarling: "Very well. I will do it. Curse you for a pack of beasts! When my people have smashed you, it will be my turn!"

"I can wait," I assured him.

Sir Roger beamed. But suddenly his face fell again. The deaf old executioner was still counting over his apparatus. "Brother Parvus," said my lord, "would you . . . could you . . . break the news to Hubert? I confess I've not the heart to tell him."

I consoled the old fellow with the thought that if Branithar were caught lying, or otherwise failing to give us honest help, there would be punishment. This sent him hobbling happily off to construct a rack. I told Branithar's guard to make sure the Wersgor saw that work.

Chapter X

At last it came time for the conference. Since most of his important followers were occupied with the study of enemy materials, Sir Roger made out a full score for his party by taking their ladies along in their finest clothes. Otherwise only a few unarmed troopers, in borrowed court panoply, accompanied him and me.

As they rode across the field toward that pergola-like structure which a Wersgor machine had erected in an hour between the two camps, of some shimmering pearly material, Sir Roger said to his wife: "I would not take you into peril like this if I had any choice. 'Tis only that we must impress them with our power and wealth."

Her face remained stony, turned from him toward the vast, sinister colunms of grounded ships. "I will be no more endangered there, my lord, than are my children back in the pavilion."

"God's name!" he groaned. "I was wrong. I should have left that cursed vessel alone and sent word to the

King. But will you hold my mistake against me all our lives?"

"They will not be long lives, thanks to your mistake," she said.

He bridled. "You swore at the wedding—"

"Oh, yes. Have I not kept my oath? I have refused you no obedience." Her cheeks flamed. "But God alone may command my feelings."

"I won't trouble you any more," he said thickly.

This I did not hear myself. They rode ahead of us all, the wind tossing their scarlet cloaks, his plumed bonnet and the veils on her conical headdress, like a picture of the perfect knight and his love. But I set it down here, conjecturally, in light of the evil luck which followed.

Being of gentle blood, Lady Catherine controlled her manner. When we drew up at the meeting place, her delicate features showed only a cold scorn, directed at the common foe. She took Sir Roger's hand and dismounted cat-graceful. He led the way more clumsily, with stormy brows.

Inside the curtained pergola was a round table, encircled by a kind of cushioned pew. The Wersgor chiefs filled one half, their snouted blue faces unreadable to us but their eyes flickering nervously. They wore metal-mesh tunics with bronze insignia of rank. In silk and vair, golden chains, ostrich plumes, cordovan hose, slashed and puffed sleeves, curl-toed shoes, the English showed like peacocks in a hen yard. I could see that the aliens were taken aback. The contrasting plainness of my friar's habit jarred them all the worse.

I folded my hands, standing, and said in the Wersgor tongue, "For the success of this parley, as well as to seal the truce, let me offer a Paternoster."

"A what?" asked the chief of the foe. He was somewhat fat, but dignified and with a strong visage.

"Silence, please." I would have explained, but their

abominable language did not seem to have any word for prayer; I had asked Branithar. *"Pater noster, qui est in coelis,"* I began, while the other English knelt with me.

I heard one of the Wersgorix mutter: "See, I told you they are barbarians. It's some superstitious ritual."

"I'm not so sure," answered the chief dubiously. "The Jairs of Boda, now, have certain formulas for psychological integration. I've seen them temporarily double their strength, or stop a wound from bleeding, or go days without sleep. Control of inner organs via the nervous system. . . . And in spite of all our own propaganda against them, you know the Jairs are as scientific as we."

I heard these clandestine exchanges readily enough, yet they did not seem aware of my awareness. I remembered now that Branithar had seemed a little deaf, too. Evidently all Wersgorix had ears less acute than men. This, I learned subsequently, was because their home planet had denser air than Terra, which made them wont to hear sounds more loudly. Here on Tharixan, with air about like England, they must raise their voices to be heard. At the time, I accepted God's gift thankfully, without stopping to wonder why nor to warn the foe.

"Amen," I finished. We all sat down at the table.

Sir Roger stabbed the chief with bleak gray eyes. "Am I dealing with a person of suitable rank?" he asked.

I translated. "What does he mean by 'rank'?" the head Wersgor wondered. "I am the governor of this planet, and these are the primary officers of its security forces."

"He means," I said, "are you sufficiently well-born that he will not demean himself by treating with you?"

They looked still more bewildered. I explained the concept of gentle birth as well as I could: which, with my limited vocabulary, was not well at all. We must thresh it over for quite some time before one of the aliens said to his lord:

"I believe I understand, *Grath* Huruga. If they know more than we do about the art of breeding for certain traits—" I must interpret many words new to me from context—"then they may have applied it to themselves. Perhaps their entire civilization is organized as a military force, with these carefully bred super-beings in command." He shuddered at the thought. "Of course, they wouldn't waste time talking to any creature of less intelligence."

Another officer exclaimed, "No, that's fantastic! In all our explorations, we've never found—"

"We have touched only the smallest fragment of the Via Galactica so far," Lord Huruga answered. "We dare not assume they are less than they claim to be, until we have more information."

I, who had sat listening to what they believed were whispers, favored them with my most enigmatic smile.

The governor said to me: "Our empire has no fixed ranks, but stations each person according to merit. I, Huruga, am the highest authority on Tharixan."

"Then I can treat with you until word has reached your emperor," said Sir Roger through me.

I had trouble with the word "emperor." Actually, the Wersgor domain was like nothing at home. Most wealthy, important persons dwelt on their vast estates with a retinue of blueface hirelings. They communicated on the far-speaker and visited in swift aircraft or spaceships. Then there were the other classes I have mentioned elsewhere, such as warriors, merchants, and politicians. But no one was born to his place in life. Under the law, all were equal, all free to strive as best they might for money or position. Indeed, they had even abandoned the idea of families. Each Wersgor lacked a surname, being identified by a number instead in a central registry. Male and female seldom lived together more than a few years. Children were sent at an early age to schools, where they dwelt until mature, for their parents oftener thought them an encumbrance than a blessing.

Yet this realm, in theory a republic of freemen, was in practice a worse tyranny than mankind has known, even in Nero's infamous day.

The Wersgorix had no special affection for their birthplace; they acknowledged no immediate ties of kinship or duty. As a result, each individual had no one to stand between him and the all-powerful central government. In England, when King John grew overweening, he clashed both with ancient law and with vested local interests; so the barons curbed him and thereby wrote another word or two of liberty for all Englishmen. The Wersgor were a lickspittle race, unable to protest any arbitrary decree of a superior. "Promotion according to merit" meant only "promotion according to one's usefulness to the imperial ministers."

But I digress, a bad habit for which my archbishop has often been forced to reprove me. I return, then, to that day in the place of nacre, when Huruga turned his terrible eyes on us and said: "It appears there are two varieties of you. Two species?"

"No," said one of his officers. "Two sexes, I'm sure. They are clearly mammals."

"Ah, yes." Huruga stared at the gowns across the table, cut low in shameless modern modes. "So I see."

When I had rendered this for Sir Roger, he said, "Tell them, in case they are curious, that our womenfolk wield swords side by side with men."

"Ah." Huruga pounced on me. "That word *sword.* Do you mean a cutting weapon?"

I had no time to ask my master's advice. I prayed inwardly for steadiness and answered, "Yes. You have observed them on our persons in camp. We find them the best tool for hand-to-hand combat. Ask any survivor of the Ganturath garrison."

"Mmm . . . yes." One of the Wersgorix looked grim. "We have neglected the tactics of infighting for centuries, *Grath* Huruga. There seemed no need for them. But I do remember one of our unofficial border clashes with the Jairs. It was out on Uloz IV, and they used long knives to wicked effect."

"For special purposes . . . yes, yes." Huruga scowled. "However, the fact remains that these invaders prance around on live animals—"

"Which need not be fueled, *Grath*, save by vegetation."

"But which could not endure a heat beam or a pellet. They wave weapons out of the prehistoric past. They come not in their own ships, but in one of ours—" He broke off his murmur and barked at me:

"See here! I've delayed long enough. Yield to our judgment, or we shall destroy you."

I interpreted. "The force screen protects us from your flame weapons," said Sir Roger. "If you wish to attack on foot, we shall make you welcome."

Huruga turned purple. "Do you imagine a force screen will stop an explosive shell?" he roared. "Why, we could lob just one, let it burst inside your screen, and wipe out every last creature of you!"

Sir Roger was less taken aback than I. "We've already heard rumors of such bursting weapons," he said to me. "Of course, he's trying to frighten us with the talk of a single shot being enough. No ship could lift so great a mass of gunpowder. Does he take me for a yokel who'll believe any tinker's yarn? However, I grant he could fire many explosive barrels into our camp."

"So what shall I tell him?" I asked fearfully.

The baron's eyes gleamed. "Render this very exactly, Brother Parvus: 'We are holding back our own artillery of this sort because we wish to talk with you, not merely kill you. If you insist on bombarding us, though, please commence. Our defenses will thwart you. Remember, however, that we are not going to keep our Wersgor prisoners inside those defenses!' "

I saw that this threat shook them. Even these hard hearts would not willingly kill some hundreds of their own people. Not that the hostages we held would stop them forever; but it was a bargaining point, which might gain us time. I wondered how we could possibly use that time, though, save to prepare our souls for death.

"Well, now," huffed Huruga, "I didn't imply I was not ready to hear you out. You have not yet told us why you have come in this unseemly, unprovoked manner."

"It was you who attacked us first, who had never harmed you," answered Sir Roger. "In England we give no dog more than one bite. My king dispatched me to teach you a lesson."

Huruga: "In one ship? Not even your own ship?"

Sir Roger: "I do not believe in bringing more than is necessary."

Huruga: "For the sake of argument, what are your demands?"

Sir Roger: "Your empire must make submission to my most puissant lord of England, Ireland, Wales, and France."

Huruga: "Let us be serious, now."

Sir Roger: "I am serious to the point of solemnity. But in order to spare further bloodshed, I'll meet any champion you name, with any weapons, to settle the issue by single combat. And may God defend the right!"

Huruga: "Are you all escaped from some mental hospital?"

Sir Roger: "Consider our position. We've suddenly discovered you, a heathen power, with arts and arms akin to ours though inferior. You could do a certain amount of harm to us, harassing our shipping or raiding our less firmly held planets. This would necessitate your extermination, and we're too merciful to enjoy that. The only sensible thing is to accept your homage."

Huruga: "And you honestly expect to—A hatful of beings, mounted on animals and swinging swords— bub-bub-bub-bub—"

He went into colloquy with his officers. "This confounded translation problem!" he complained. "I'm never sure if I've understood them aright. They *could* be a punitive expedition, I suppose. For reasons of military secrecy, they *could* have used one of our own ships and kept their most potent weapons in reserve. It doesn't make sense. But neither does it make sense that barbarians would blandly tell the most powerful realm in the known universe to surrender its autonomy. Unless it's mere bluster. But we may be completely misunderstanding their demands . . . and thereby misjudging them, perhaps to our own serious loss. Hasn't anyone got any ideas?"

Meanwhile I said to Sir Roger, "You aren't serious about this, my lord?"

Lady Catherine could not resist saying: "He would be."

"Nay." The baron shook his head. "Of course not. What would King Edward do with a lot of unruly bluefaces? The Irish are bad enough. Nay, I hope only to let myself be bargained down. If we can wring from them some guarantee to let Terra alone—and perhaps a few coffers of gold for ourselves—"

"And guidance home," I said gloomily.

"That's a riddle we must think on later," he snapped. "No time now. Certainly we dare not admit to the enemy that we're waifs."

Huruga turned back to us. "You must realize your demand is preposterous," he said. "However, if you can demonstrate that your realm is worth the trouble, our emperor will be glad to receive an ambassador from it."

Sir Roger yawned and said languidly, through me:

"Spare your insults. My monarch will receive your emissary, perhaps, if that person adopts the true Faith."

"What is this *Faith?*" asked Huruga, for again I must use an English word.

"The true belief, of course," I said. "The facts about Him who is the source of all wisdom and righteousness, and to whom we humbly pray for guidance."

"What's he babbling about now, *Grath?*" muttered an officer.

"I don't know," Huruga whispered back. "Perhaps these, uh, English maintain some kind of giant computing engine to which they submit the important questions for decision. . . . I don't know. Confounded translation problem! Best we delay awhile. Watch them, their behavior; mull over what we've heard."

"And dispatch a message to Wersgorixan?"

"No, you fool! Not yet, not till we know more. Do you want the main office to think we can't handle our own problems? If these really are mere barbarian pirates, can you imagine what would happen to all our careers if we called in the whole navy?"

Huruga turned to me and said aloud: "We have ample time for discussion. Let us adjourn until tomorrow, and think well in the meantime on every implication."

Sir Roger was glad of that. "Let's make certain of the truce terms, though," he added.

I was getting more facility in the Wersgor language with every hour, so I was soon able to elucidate that their concept of a truce was not ours. Their insatiable hunger for land made them the enemy of all other races, so they could not imagine a binding oath exchanged with anyone not blue and tailed.

The armistice was no formal agreement at all, but a statement of temporary mutual convenience. They declared that they did not at present find it expedient to fire on us, even when we grazed our kine beyond the force screen. This condition would prevail as long as we refrained from attacking any of them who moved about in the open. For fear of espionage and missile dropping, neither side wished the other to fly within view of the camps, and would shoot at any vessel which lifted. That was all. They would surely violate this if they decided it was to their interest; they would work us harm if they saw any method of doing so; and they expected us to feel likewise.

"They have the better of it, sire," I mourned. "All our flying craft are here. Now we can't even jump into our spaceships and flee; they'd pounce ere we could elude pursuit. Whereas they have many other ships, elsewhere on the planet, which may hover freely beyond the horizon and be ready to assail us when the time comes."

"Nevertheless," said Sir Roger, "I perceive certain advantages. This business of neither giving nor expecting pledges—aye—"

"It suits you," murmured Lady Catherine.

He whitened, leaped to his feet, bowed at Huruga, and led us out.

Chapter XI

The long afternoon allowed our people to make considerable progress. With Branithar to instruct them, or to interpret for those prisoners who understood the art in question, the English soon mastered the controls of many devices. They practiced with spaceships and small flying vessels, being careful to raise these only a few inches off the ground, lest the foe observe it and shoot. They also drove about in horseless wagons; they learned to use far-speakers, magnifying optical devices, and other esoterica; they handled weapons that threw fire, or metal, or invisible stunning beams. Of course we English had, as yet, no inkling of the occult knowledge which had gone into making such things. But we found them childishly simple to use. At home, we harnessed animals, wound intricate crossbows and catapults, rigged sailing ships, erected machines by which human muscles might raise heavy stones. This business of twisting a wheel or pulling a lever was naught in comparison. The only real difficulty was for unlettered yeomen to remember what the symbols on the gauges stood for—and this, indeed, was no more complicated a science than heraldry, which any hero-worshiping lad could rattle off in detail.

Being the only person with pretensions to reading the Wersgor alphabet, I busied myself with papers seized in the fortress offices. Meanwhile Sir Roger conferred with his captains and directed the most oafish serfs, who could not learn the new weapons, in certain construction work. The slow sunset was burning, turning half the sky gold, when he summoned me to his council board.

I seated myself and looked at those gaunt hard faces. They were animated with fresh hope. My tongue clove to my mouth. Well I knew these captains. Most of all did I know how Sir Roger's eyes danced—when hell was being hatched!

"Have you learned what and where the principal castles of this planet are, Brother Parvus?" he asked me.

"Yes, sire," I told him. "There are but three, of which Ganturath was one."

"I can't believe that!" exclaimed Sir Owain Montbelle. "Why, pirates alone would—"

"You forget there are no separate kingdoms here, or even separate fiefs," I answered. "All persons are directly subservient to the imperial government. The fortresses are only lodging for the sheriffs, who keep order among the populace and collect the taxes. True, these fortresses are also supposed to be defensive bases. They include docks for the great star ships, and warriors are stationed there. But the Wersgorix have fought no true war for a long time. They've merely bullied helpless savages. None of the other star-traveling races dare declare open war on them; only now and then does a skirmish occur on some remote planet. In short, three fortresses are ample for this whole world."

"How strong are they?" snapped Sir Roger.

"There is one hight Stularax, on the other side of the globe, which is about like Ganturath. Then there is the main fortress, Darova, where this proconsul Huruga dwells. That one is by far the largest and strongest. I daresay it supplied most of the ships and warriors we see facing us."

"Where is the next world inhabited by bluefaces?"

"According to a book I studied, about twenty light-years hence. Wersgorixan itself, the capital planet, is much farther off than that—farther away than Terra, even."

"But the far-speaker would inform their emperor at once of what's happened, would it not?" asked Captain Bullard.

"No," I said. "The far-speaker acts only as fast as light. Messages between the stars must go by space-ship, which means that it would take a brace of weeks to inform Wersgorixan. Not that Huruga has done so. I overheard him speak to one of his court, to say they would keep this affair secret awhile."

"Aye," said Sir Brian Fitz-William. "The duke will seek to redeem himself for what we have done, by crushing us unaided ere he reports anything whatsoever. 'Tis a common enough way of thinking."

"If we hurt him badly enough, though, he'll scream for help," prophesied Sir Owain.

"Just so," agreed Sir Roger. "And I've thought of a way to hurt him!"

I realized gloomily that when my tongue had cloven to my mouth it knew what it was doing.

"How can we fight?" asked Bullard. "We've no amount of devil-weapons to compare with what sits out on yon field. If need be, they could ram us, boat for boat, and count it no great loss."

"For which reason," Sir Roger told him, "I propose a raid on the smaller fort, Stularax, to gain more weapons. 'Twill also jar Huruga out of his confidence."

"Or jar him into attacking us."

" 'Tis a chance we must take. Come worst to worst, I'm not altogether terrified of another fight. See you not, our *only* chance is to act with boldness."

There was no great demurral. Sir Roger had had hours in which to jolly his folk. They were ready enough to accept his leadership again. But Sir Brian objected sensibly: "How can we effect any such raid? Yon castle lies thousands of miles hence. We cannot flit thither from our camp without being fired upon."

Sir Owain raised mocking brows. "Maybe you've a magic horse?" He smiled at Sir Roger.

"No. Another sort of beast. Hearken to me. . . ."

That was a long night's work for the yeomen. They put skids under one of the smaller spaceboats, hitched oxen to it, and dragged it forth as quietly as might be. Its passage across open fields was disguised by driving cattle around it, as if grazing them. Under cover of darkness, and by God's grace, the ruse was sufficient. Once beneath the tall thick-crowned trees, with a screen of scouts who moved like shadows to warn of any blue soldiers—"They had the practice for it, poaching at home," said Red John—the work was safer but also more hard. Not until nearly dawn was the boat several miles from camp, so far off that it could lift without being seen from Huruga's field headquarters.

Though the largest vessel which could possibly be moved thus, it was still too small to carry the most formidable weapons. However, Sir Roger had during the day examined the explosive shells fired by certain types of gun. He had had it explained to him by a terrified Wersgor engineer, how to arm the fuse thereon, so that it would go off on impact. The boat carried several of these—also a disassembled trebuchet which his artisans had constructed.

Meanwhile, everyone not toiling with this was set to work strengthening our camp defenses. Even women and children were given shovels. Axes rang in the near-by forest. Long as the night was, it seemed even longer when we labored thus exhaustingly, stopping only to snatch a piece of bread or a wink of sleep. The Wersgorix observed that we were busy—it could not be avoided—but we tried to conceal from them what we actually did, lest they see we were merely ringing the lesser half of Ganturath with stakes, pits, caltrops, and chevaux-de-frise. When morning came, with full daylight, our installations were hidden from view by the long grass.

I myself welcomed such backbreaking labor as a surcease from my fears. Yet my mind must worry them, like a dog with a bone. Was Sir Roger mad? There seemed to be so many things he had done awry. Yet, to each successive question, I found only the same answer as himself.

Why had we not fled the moment we possessed Ganturath, instead of waiting till Huruga arrived and pinned us down? Because we had lost the way home and had no chance whatsoever of finding it without the help of skilled space sailors. (If it could be found at all.) Death was better than a blind blundering among the stars—where our ignorance would soon kill us anyway.

Having gained a truce, why did Sir Roger run the gravest risk of its immediate breach by this attack on Stularax? Because it was plain the truce could not last very long. Given time to ponder what he had observed, Huruga must see through our pretensions and destroy us. Thrown off balance by our boldness, he might well continue to believe us more powerful than was the truth. Or if he elected to fight, we should have our hands strengthened by whatever arms were seized in the forthcoming raid.

But did Sir Roger seriously expect so mad a plan to succeed? Only God and himself could answer that. I knew he was improvising as he went along. He was like a runner who stumbles and must all at once run even faster so as not to fall.

But how splendidly he ran!

That reflection soothed me. I committed my fate to Heaven and shoveled with a more peaceful heart.

Just before dawn, as mist streamed among buildings and tents and long-snouted fire-bombards, under the first thin light creeping up the sky, Sir Roger saw his raiders off. They were twenty: Red John with the best of our yeomen, and Sir Owain Montbelle as chief. It was curious how that knight's often faint heart always revived at the prospect of action. He was almost gay as a boy when he stood there wrapped in a long scarlet cloak, listening to his orders.

"Go through the woods, keeping well under cover, to where the boat lies," my lord told him. "Wait till noon, then fly off. You know how to use those unrolling maps for guide, eh? Well, then, when you come to this Stularax place—'twill take an hour or so if you fly at what seems a reasonable speed hereabouts—land where you have cover. Give it a few shells from the trebuchet to reduce the outer defenses. Dash in afoot, while they're still confused; seize what you can from the arsenals, and return. If all is still peaceful hereabouts, lie quietly. If fighting has broken out, well, do what seems best."

"Indeed, sire." Sir Owain clasped his hand. That gesture was not fated to occur between them again.

As they stood there under darkling skies, a voice called: "Wait." All the men turned their faces toward the inner buildings, where mist smoked thickly. Out of it came the Lady Catherine.

"I have only now heard you were going," she said to Sir Owain. "Must you—twenty men against a fortress?"

"Twenty men—" He bowed, with a smile that lit his face like the sun—"and myself, and the memory of you, my lady!"

The color crept up her pale countenance. She walked past a stone-stiff Sir Roger, to the younger knight, till she stood gazing up at him. All saw that her hands bled. She held a cord in them.

"After I could no more lift a spade this night," she whispered, "I helped twine bowstrings. I can give you no other token."

Sir Owain accepted it in a great silence. Having laid it within his shirt of chain mail, he kissed her scarred small fingers. Straightening, his cloak aswirl about him, he led his yeomen into the forest.

Sir Roger had not moved. Lady Catherine nodded a little. "And you are going to sit at table today with the Wersgorix?" she asked him.

She slipped away in the fog, back toward the pavilion which he no longer shared. He waited until she was quite out of sight before following.

Chapter XII

Our people made good use of the long morning to rest themselves. By now I could read Wersgor clocks, though not precisely sure how their units of time compared to Terrestrial hours. At high noon I mounted my palfrey and met Sir Roger to go to the conference. He was alone. "Methought we were to be a score," I faltered.

His countenance was wooden. "No more reason for that," he said. "It may go ill for us in yon rendezvous, when Huruga learns of the raid. I'm sorry I must hazard you."

I was sorry, too, but wished not to spend time in self-pity which could be more usefully devoted to telling my beads.

The same Wersgor officers awaited us within the pearly curtains. Huruga looked his surprise as we trod in. "Where are your other negotiators?" he asked sharply.

"At their prayers," I replied, which was belike true enough.

"There goes that word again," grumbled one of the blueskins. "What does it *mean?*"

"Thus." I illustrated by saying an Ave and marking it off on my rosary.

"Some kind of calculating machine, I think," said another Wersgor, "It may not be as primitive as it looks on the outside, either."

"But what does it calculate?" whispered a third one, his ears raised straight up with uneasiness.

Huruga glared. "This has gone far enough," he snapped. "All night you were at work over there. If you plan some trick—"

"Don't you wish you had a plan?" I interrupted in my most Christianly sweet voice.

As I hoped, this insolence rocked him back. We sat down.

After chewing on it a moment, Huruga exclaimed: "About your prisoners. I am responsible for the safety of residents of this planet. I cannot possibly treat with creatures who hold Wersgorix captive. The first condition of any further negotiations must be their immediate release."

" 'Tis a shame we cannot negotiate, then," said Sir Roger via myself. "I don't really want to destroy you."

"You shall not leave this place until those captives are delivered to me," said Huruga. I gasped. He smiled coldly. "I have soldiers on call, in case you, too, brought something like this." He reached in his tunic and pulled out a pellet-throwing handgun. I stared down the muzzle and gulped.

Sir Roger yawned. He buffed his nails on a silken sleeve. "What did he say?" he asked me.

I told him. "Treachery," I groaned. "We were all supposed to be unarmed."

"Nay, remember no oaths were sworn. But tell his disgrace Duke Huruga that I foresaw this chance, and carry my own protection." The baron pressed the ornate seal ring on his finger, and clenched his fist. "I have cocked it now. If my hand unclasps for any reason before 'tis uncocked again, the stone will burst with enough force to send us all flying past St. Peter."

Through clattering teeth, I got this mendacious message out. Huruga sprang to his feet. "Is this true?" he roared.

"I-i-indeed it is," I said. "B-b-by Mahomet I swear it."

The blue officers huddled together. From their frantic whispers I gathered that a bombshell as tiny as that sealstone was possible in theory, though no race known to the Wersgorix were skillful enough to make one.

Calm prevailed at last. "Well," said Huruga, "it looks like an impasse. I myself think you're lying, but do not care to risk my life." He slipped the little gun back in his tunic. "However, you must realize this is an impossible situation. If I can't obtain the release of those prisoners myself, I shall be forced to refer this whole matter to the Imperium on Wersgorixan."

"You need not be so hasty," Sir Roger told him. "We'll keep our hostages carefully. You may send chirurgeons to look after their health. To be sure, we must ask you to sequestrate all your armament, as a guarantee of good faith. But in return, we'll mount guard against the Saracens."

"The what?" Huruga wrinkled his bony forehead.

"The Saracens. Heathen pirates. You've not encountered them? I find that hard to believe, for they range widely. Why, at this very minute a Saracen ship could be descending on your own planet, to pillage and burn—"

Huruga jerked. He pulled an officer aside and whispered to him. This time I could not follow what was said. The officer hurried out.

"Tell me more," said Huruga.

"With pleasure." The baron leaned back in his seat. at cross-legged ease. I could never have achieved his calm. As nearly as I could gauge, Sir Owain's boat must now be at Stularax; for recall how much slower this conversation was than I have written it, with all the translation, the pauses to explain some uncomprehended word, the search for a telling phrase.

Yet Sir Roger spun out his yarn as if he had eternity. He explained that we English had fallen so savagely upon the Wersgorix because their unprovoked attack led us to think they must be new allies of the Saracens. Now that we understood otherwise, it was possible that in time England and Wersgorixan could reach agreement, alliance against this common menace. . . .

The blue officer dashed back inside. Through the door flap I saw soldiery in the alien camp hurrying to their posts; a roar of awakening machines came to my ears.

"Well?" Huruga barked at his underling.

"Reports—the far-speaker—outlying homes saw bright flash—Stularax gone—must have been a shell of the superpowered type—" The fellow blurted it out between his pantings.

Sir Roger exchanged a look with me as I translated. Stularax gone? Utterly destroyed?

Our aim had only been to reave some more weapons, especially light portable ones for our men-at-arms. But if everything had vanished in smoke . . .

Sir Roger licked dry lips. "Tell him the Saracens must have landed, Brother Parvus," he said.

Huruga gave me no chance. Breast heaving with wrath, amber eyes turned blood-red, he stood shaking, pulled out his handgun again and screamed: "No more of this farce! Who else was with you? How many more spaceships have you?"

Sir Roger uncoiled himself, till he loomed above the stumpy Wersgorix like an oak on a heath. He grinned, touched his signet ring meaningfully, and said: "Well, now, you can't expect me to reveal that. Perhaps I'd best return to my camp, till your temper has cooled."

I could not phrase it so smoothly in my halting words. Huruga snarled: "Oh, no! Here you stay!"

"I go." Sir Roger shook his close-cropped head. "Incidentally, if for any reason I don't return, my men have orders to kill all the prisoners."

Huruga heard me out. With a self-mastery I admired, he replied: "Go, then. But when you are back, we shall attack you. I do not propose to be caught between your camp on the ground and your friends in the sky."

"The hostages," Sir Roger reminded him.

"We shall attack," repeated Huruga doggedly. "It will be entirely with ground forces—partly to spare those same prisoners, and partly, of course, because every spaceship and aircraft must get aloft and search for those attackers of Stularax. We will also refrain from using high-explosive weapons, lest we destroy the captives. *But*—" He stabbed a finger down upon the table. "Unless your weapons are far superior to what I think, we will overwhelm you with sheer numbers, if nothing else. I don't believe you even have any armored wagons, only a few light ground cars captured at Ganturath. Remember, after the battle, such of your folk as survive will be our prisoners. If you have harmed a single one of those Wersgorix you hold, your people will die, very slowly. If you yourself are caught alive, Sir Roger de Tourneville, you will watch all of them die before you do yourself."

The baron heard me render this for him. The lips were very pale in his sunburned face. "Well, Brother Parvus," he said in rather a small voice, "it's not worked out as well as I hoped—though perhaps not quite as badly as I feared. Tell him that if he will indeed let us two return safely, and confine his attack to ground forces, and avoid high-explosive shells, our hostages shall be safe from anything but his own fire."

He added wryly: "I don't think I could have made

myself butcher helpless captives anyhow. But you need not tell him that."

Huruga merely jerked his head, an icy gesture, when I gave him the message. We two humans left, swung into the saddle and turned back. We held our horses to a walk, to prolong the truce and the feel of sunlight on our faces.

"What happened at that Stularax castle, sire?" I whispered.

"I know not," said Sir Roger. "But I'll hazard that the blue-faces spoke truly—and I didn't believe it!—when they said one of their more powerful shells could wipe out an encampment. So the weapons we hoped to steal are gone. I can only pray that our poor raiders were not also caught in the blast. Now we can but defend ourselves."

He raised his plumed head. "Yet Englishmen have ever fought best with their backs to the wall."

Chapter XIII

So we rode into camp, and my lord shouted haro as if this battle had been his dearest wish. In a great iron clangor, our folk went to their stations.

Let me describe our situation more fully. As a minor base, Ganturath was not built to withstand the most powerful forces of war. The lesser portion, which we occupied, consisted of several low masonry buildings arranged in a circle. Outside that circle were the armored emplacements of the fire-bombards; but these, being meant only to shoot upward at skycraft, were useless to us now. Underground was a warren of rooms and passages. There we put our children, aged, prisoners, and cattle, in charge of a few armed serfs. Such older people, or others not fit for combat, as were spry enough, waited near the middle of the buildings, prepared to carry off the wounded, fetch beer, and otherwise aid the fighting line.

This line stood on the side facing the Wersgor camp, just within the low earthen wall erected during the night. Their pikes, bills, and axes were reinforced at intervals by squads of bowmen. The cavalry poised at either wing. Behind them were the younger women and certain untrained men, who shared out our all too few pellet weapons; the force screen made fire guns useless.

Around us shimmered the pale heat-lightning of that shield. Behind us rose the ancient forest. Before us, bluish grass rippled down the valley, isolated trees soughed, and clouds walked above the distant hills. It all had the eerie loveliness of a landscape in Faerie. Preparing bandages with the aboveground noncombatants, I wondered why there must be hatred and killing in so sweet a realm.

Flying craft thundered skyward and out of sight from the Wersgor camp. Our gunners dropped a few ere they were all gone. A number remained on the ground, held in reserve. They included some of the very largest transport ships. At the moment, however, my chief interest was the ground.

Wersgorix streamed forth, armed with long-barreled pellet weapons and in well-ordered squads. They did not advance in close ranks but scattered as much as possible. Some of our folk let out a cheer at this, but I knew it must be their ordinary ground-fighting tactics. When one has deadly rapid-fire guns, one does not attack in solid masses. Rather, one employs devices to take the enemy's guns out of action.

Such engines were in fact present. Doubtless they had been flown hither from the central bastion of Darova. There were two kinds of these horseless warwagons. The most numerous sort was light and open, made of thin steel, holding four soldiers and a couple of rapid-fire weapons. They ran immensely fast and agile, like water beetles on four wheels. As I saw them whip and scream about, bouncing at a hundred miles an hour over broken terrain, I understood their purpose: to be so difficult to hit that most of them could work up to the very bombards of the foe.

However, these small cars hung back, covering the Wersgor infantry. The first line of actual attack was the heavy-armored vehicles. These moved but slowly for a powered machine, no faster than a horse could gallop. This was because of their size—big as a peasant's cottage—and the thick steel plating which could withstand all but a direct shellburst. With bombards projecting from their turrets, with their roaring and dust, they were like unto dragons. I counted more than twenty: massive, impervious, grinding forward on treads in a wide line. Where they had passed, grass and earth were smashed into stone-hard ruts.

I am told that one of our gunners, who had learned how to use the wheeled cannon which threw explosive shells, broke ranks and dashed for such a weapon. Sir Roger himself, now armed cap-a-pie, rode up and knocked him asprawl with his lance. "Hold on, there!" rapped the baron. "What're you about?"

"To shoot, sire," gasped the soldier. "Let's fire at 'em ere they break over our wall and—"

"If I didn't think our good yew bows could deal with such overgrown snails, I'd have you priming yon tube," said my lord. "But as it is, back to your pike!"

It had a salutary effect on the badly shaken spearmen, who stood with weapons grounded to receive that frightful charge. Sir Roger saw no reason to explain that (judging from what had happened at Stularax) he dared not use explosives at such short range, lest he destroy us, too. Of course, he should have realized that the Wersgorix would have many kinds of shell of graded potency. But who can think of everything at once?

As it was, the drivers of those moving fortresses must have been sorely puzzled that we did not fire on them, and wondered what we held in reserve. They found out when the first war-wagon toppled into one of our covered pits.

Two more were similarly trapped ere it was understood that these were no ordinary obstacles. Surely the good saints had aided us. In our ignorance, we had dug holes broad and deep, which by themselves would not have been escape-proof for such powerful vehicles. But then we added great wooden stakes, almost by sheer habit, as if we expected to impale outsize horses. Some of these caught in the treads which girdled the wheels, and erelong those wheels were jammed tight with wood pulp.

Another wagon evaded the pits, which were not continuous. It approached the breastworks. A rapid-fire gun spat from it, seeking the range, and stitched small craters along our earth wall. "God send the right!" roared Sir Brian Fitz-William. His horse spurted from our lines, closely followed by half a dozen of the nearer cavalrymen. They galloped in a semicircle, just beyond reach of the gun. The vehicle lumbered in pursuit, seeking to bring its smallest-bore cannon to bear. Sir Brian got it headed the way he desired, winded his war-horn, and galloped back to shelter as the wagon plunged into a hole.

The war-turtles drew back. In that long grass, and with our cunning camouflage, they had no way of knowing where the other traps were. And these were the only such machines on all Tharixan, not to be lightly hazarded. We English had trembled lest they continue. Only one would have had to get through to wipe us out.

Even though his information about us, our powers, and our possible spaceborne reinforcements was scanty, I think Huruga should have ordered the heavy wagons onward. Indeed, the Wersgor tactics were deplorable in all respects. But remember that for a long time they had not fought seriously on the ground. Their conquest of backward planets was a mere battue; their skirmishes with rival starfaring nations were mostly aerial.

Thus Huruga, discouraged by our pits but heartened by our failure to use low-power shellfire, withdrew the great cars. Instead, he sent the infantry and the light vehicles against us. His idea was plainly for them to find a path between our traps and mark it for the giant machines to follow.

The blue soldiers came at a run, scarcely visible through the tall grass, divided into little squads. I myself, being placed far back, saw only the occasional flash of a helmet and the poles which they stuck up here and there to mark a safe channel for the heavy wagons. Yet I knew they numbered many thousands. My heart thudded within me, and my mouth longed for a beaker of ale.

Ahead of the soldiers came racing the light cars. A few of them went into pits and at such speeds were horribly wrecked. But most sped in a straight line—straight into the stakes we had planted in the grass near our breastworks, in case of a cavalry charge.

So fast were they traveling, the cars were almost as vulnerable to such a defense as horses would be. I saw one rise in the air, turn over, smash back to earth, and bounce twice ere it broke apart. I saw another impale itself, spout liquid fuel, and burst into flame. I saw a third swerve, skid, and crash into a fourth.

Several more, escaping the abatis, ran over the caltrops we had scattered around. The iron spikes entered the soft rings encircling their wheels and were not to be gotten out. A car so injured could at best limp feebly from the battle.

Commands in the harsh Wersgor tongue must have rattled over the far-speaker. The majority of the open cars, still unscathed, ceased to mill about. They drew into a loose but orderly formation, and advanced at a walking pace.

Snap! went our catapults and *crash!* went our ballistae. Bolts, stones, and pots of burning oil hailed atrociously among the advancing vehicles. Not many were thus disabled, but their line wavered and slowed.

Then our cavalry charged.

A few of our horsemen died, caught in a storm of lead. But they had not far to gallop to reach the enemy. Also, the grass fires started by our oil pots confused Wersgor vision with their heavy smoke. I heard a clang and boom as lances burst against iron sides, then had no more chance to watch that struggle. I know only that the lancers failed to disable any car with their shafts. However, it startled the drivers so much that these often failed completely to defend themselves against what followed. Rearing horses brought down hoofs, to crumple the thin steel plates; a few quick swipes of ax, mace, or sword emptied a vehicle of its crew. Some of Sir Roger's men used handguns to good effect, or small round shells which burst and scattered jagged fragments when thrown after a pin was released. The Wersgorix had similar weapons, of course, but less determination to use them.

The last cars fled in terror, hotly pursued by the English riders. "Come back, there!" bellowed Sir Roger at them. He shook the fresh lance given him by his esquire. "Come back, you caitiff rogues! Stand and deliver, you base-born heathen!" He must have been a splendid sight, gleaming metal and fluttering plumage and blazoned shield upon the restless coal-black stallion. But the Wersgorix were not a knightly folk. They were more prudent and forethoughtful than we. It cost them dearly.

Our horsemen must quickly retreat, for now the blue foot was close, firing their guns as they pulled into larger masses for the assault on our breastworks. Armor was no protection, only a bright target. Sir Roger bugled his men to follow him, and they scattered out onto the plain.

The Wersgorix set up a defiant cheer and rushed. Across the seething confusion of our camp, I heard the archer captains howl their command. Then the gray goose flock went skyward with a noise as of mighty winds.

It came down, gruesomely, among the Wersgorix. While the first arrow flight was still rising, the second was on its way. A shaft with so much force behind it pierces the body and comes out on the other side with its broad cutting head all bloody. And now the crossbows, slower but still more powerful, began to mow down the nearest attackers. I think that during those last few moments of their charge, the Wersgorix must have lost half their folk.

Nonetheless, dogged almost as Englishmen, they ran on to our very wall. And here our common men-at-arms stood to receive them. The women fired and fired, pinning down a goodly part of the foe. Those who came so close that guns were useless, must face ax, spear, billhook, mace, morningstar, dagger, and broadsword.

Despite their awesome losses, the Wersgorix still outnumbered our folk two or three to one. Yet it was scarcely fair. They had no body armor. Their only weapon for such close-in fighting was a knife attached to the muzzle of the handgun, to make a most awkward spear ... or the gun itself, clubbed. A few did carry pellet-firing sidearms, which caused us some casualties. But as a rule, when John Blueface fired at Harry Englishman, he missed even at pointblank range, in all that turmoil. Before John could fire again, Harry had laid him open with a halberd.

When our cavalry returned, striking the Wersgor infantry from the rear and hewing away, it was the end. The enemy broke and ran, trampling his own comrades in blind horror. The riders chased them, with merry hunting calls. When they were far enough away, our longbows cut loose once more.

Still, many escaped who must otherwise have been spitted on a lance, for Sir Roger saw the heavy wagons trundling vengefully back and retreated with his folk. By God's mercy, I was so occupied caring for the wounded fetched to me that I knew nothing of that moment when our leaders thought we were undone after all. For the Wersgor charge had not gone for naught. It had succeeded in showing the turtle-cars how to avoid our pits. And now the iron giants came across a field turned into red mud, and naught we knew could stop them.

Thomas Bullard's shoulders slumped where he sat mounted near the baronial pennon. "Well," he sighed, "we gave what was ours to give. Now who will ride out with me to show them how Englishmen can die?"

Sir Roger's weary face drew into grave lines. "We've a harder task than that, friends," he said. "We were right to hazard our lives on a chance of victory. Now that we see defeat upon us, we've no right to throw those lives away. We must live—as slaves, if need be—so that our women and babes are not altogether alone on this hell-world."

"God's bones!" shouted Sir Brian Fitz-William. "Are you gone craven?"

The baron's nostrils flared. "You heard me," he said. "We stay here."

And then—lo! It was as if God Himself had come to deliver His poor sinful partisans. Brighter than lightning, a blue-white flash burst, several miles off in the forest. So lurid was the radiance that those few who chanced to be looking in that direction were blind for hours afterward. No doubt a great many Wersgorix were thus incapacitated, since their army faced it. The roar that followed knocked riders from their saddles and men from their feet. A wind swept us all, furnace hot, and carried tents before it like blown rags. Then, as that shattering wrath departed, we saw a cloud of dust and smoke arise. Shaped like an evil mushroom it towered almost to heaven. Minutes passed before it began to dissipate; its upper clouds lingered for hours.

The charging war-cars ground to a halt, They knew, as we did not, what that burst signified. It was a shell of the ultimate potency, that destruction of matter which I cannot but feel to this day is an impious tampering with God's work, though my archbishop has cited me Scriptural texts to prove that any art is lawful if it be used for good purposes.

This was not a very strong shell, as such weapons go. It was meant to annihilate a half-mile circle, and produced comparatively little of those subtle poisons which accompany such explosions. And it had been fired distantly enough from the scene of action to harm no one.

Yet it put the Wersgorix in a cruel dilemma. If they used a similar weapon to wipe out our camp—if they overran us by any means—they might expect a hail of death. For the hidden bombard would have no further reason to spare the area of Ganturath. Thus they must suspend their assault upon us, until they had found and dealt with this new enemy.

Their war-wagons lumbered back. Most of the aircraft they had in reserve lifted and scattered widely, searching for whoever had fired that shell. The chief implement of this search was (as we knew from our own studies) a device embodying the same forces as are found in lodestone. Through powers which I do not understand, and have no desire to understand since the knowledge is unessential to salvation if not smacking of the black arts, this device could smell out large metallic masses. A gun big enough to fire a shell of the known potency should have been discovered by any aircraft flitting within a mile of its hiding place.

Yet no such gun could be located. After a tense hour, while we English watched and prayed on our walls, Sir Roger gusted a deep breath.

"I don't want to seem ungrateful," he said, "but I

do believe God's helped us through Sir Owain, rather than directly. We ought to find his party somewhere out in the woods, even if those enemy flyers don't seem able to. Father Simon, you must know who the best poachers are in your parish—"

"Oh, my son!" exclaimed the chaplain.

Sir Roger grinned. "I ask for no secrets of the confessional. I'm only telling you to appoint a few ... shall we say, skilled woodsmen? ... to sneak their way through the grass into yon forest. Have them locate Sir Owain, wherever he is, and order him to hold his fire till I send word. You needn't tell me who you appoint, Father."

"In that case, my son, it shall be as you command." The priest drew me aside and asked me to give spiritual comfort to the injured and frightened as his *locum tenens,* while he led a small scout party into the forest.

But my lord found another task for me. He and I and an esquire rode out under a white banner toward the Wersgor camp. We assumed the foe would have wit enough to understand our meaning, even if they did not use the same truce signal. And thus it was. Huruga himself drove out in an open car to meet us. His blue jowls looked shrunken, and his hands trembled.

"I call upon you to yield," said the baron. "Stop forcing me to destroy your poor benighted commoners. I pledge you'll all be treated fairly and allowed to write home for ransom money."

"I, yield to a barbarian like you?" croaked the Wersgor. "Just because you have some ... some confounded detection-proof cannon—no!" He paused. "But to get rid of you, I'll allow you to leave in the spaceships you've seized."

"Sire." I gasped when I had translated this, "have we indeed won escape?"

"Hardly," Sir Roger answered. "We can't find our way back, remember; and as yet, we dare not ask for a skilled navigator to help us, or we'd reveal our weakness and be attacked again. Even if we did somehow win home, 'twould still leave this nest of devils free to plot a renewed assault on England. Nay, I fear that he who mounts a bear cannot soon dismount."

So with a heavy heart, I told the blue noble that we had come for more than some of his shoddy, old-fashioned spaceships, and if he did not surrender we would be forced to devastate his land. Huruga snarled for reply and drove back.

We also returned. Presently Red John Hameward came from the forest with Father Simon's party, which he had encountered on his way to our camp.

"We flew to that Stularax castle openly, sire," he related. "We saw other sky-boats, but none challenged us, taking us for a simple ship o' their own. Still, we knew no fortress sentries'd let us land without some questions. So we put down in some woods, a few miles from the keep. We set up our trebuchet and put one o' those bursting shells in't. Sir Owain's idea was to lob a few to shake up their outer defenses. Then we'd slip closer afoot, leaving a crew to fire some more shells when we was near and break down their walls. We expected the garrison'd be scurrying about in search of our engine, so we could slip in, kill whatever guards were left behind, lift what we could carry from their arsenal, and return to our boat."

At this point, since it is no longer used, I had best explain the trebuchet. It was the simplest but in many ways the most effective siege engine. In principle it was only a great lever, freely swinging on some fulcrum. A very long arm ended in a bucket for the missile, while the short arm bore a stone weight, often of several tons. This latter was raised by pulleys or a winch, while the bucket was loaded. Then the weight was released, and in falling it swung the long arm through a mighty arc.

"I didn't think much o' those shells we had," Red

John went on. "Why, the things didn't weigh no more'n five pounds. We'd trouble rigging the trebuchet to cast 'em only those few miles. And what could they do, I wondered, but burst with a pop? I've seen trebuchets used proper, laying siege to French cities. We'd throw boulders of a ton or two, or sometimes dead horses, over the walls. But, well, orders was orders. So I m'self cocked the little shell like I'd been told how to, and we let fly. Whoom! The world blew up, like. I had to admit this was even better to throw nor a dead horse.

"Well, through the magnifying screens we could see the castle was pretty much flattened. No use raiding it now. We lobbed a few more shells to make sure it were reduced proper. Nothing there now but a big glassy pit. Sir Owain reckoned as we was carrying a weapon more useful nor any which we could o' lifted, and I'd say he were right. So we landed in the woods some miles hence and dragged the trebuchet forth and set it up again. That's what took us so long, m' lord. When Sir Owain had seen from the air what was happening about that time, we fired a shell just to scare the enemy a bit. Now we're ready to pound 'em as much as you wish, sire."

"But the boat?" asked Sir Roger. "The foe have metal-sniffers. That's why they haven't found your trebuchet in the forest: it's made of wood. But surely they could discover your flying boat, wherever you've hid it."

"Oh, that, sire." Red John grinned. "Sir Owain's got our boat flitting up there 'mongst t'others. Who's to tell the difference in yon swarm?"

Sir Roger whooped laughter. "You missed a glorious fight," he said, "but you can light the balefire. Go back and tell your men to start shelling the enemy camp."

We withdrew underground at the agreed-on moment, as shown on captured Wersgor timepieces. Even so, we felt the earth shudder, and heard the dull roaring, as their ground installations and most of their ground machines were destroyed. A single shot was enough. The survivors thereof stormed in blind terror aboard one of the transport ships, abandoning much perfectly unharmed equipment. The lesser sky-craft were even quicker to vanish, like blown sea scud. As the slow sunset began to burn in that direction we had wistfully named the west, England's leopards flew above England's victory.

Chapter XIV

Sir Owain landed like some hero of a chanson come to earth. His exploits had not required much effort of him. While buzzing around in the middle of the Wersgor air fleet, he had even heated water over a brazier and shaved. Lithely now he walked, head erect, mailcoat shining, red cloak aflutter in the wind. Sir Roger met him near the knightly tents, battered, filthy, reeking, clotted with blood. His voice was hoarse from shouting. "My compliments, Sir Owain, on a most gallant action."

The younger man swept him a bow—and changed it most subtly to Lady Catherine's, as she emerged from our cheering throng. "I could have done no less," murmured Sir Owain, "with a bowstring about my heart."

The color mounted to her face. Sir Roger's eyes flickered from one to another. Indeed, they made a fair couple. I saw his hands clench on the haft of his nicked and blunted sword.

"Go to your tent, madame," he told his wife.

"There is still work to do among the wounded, sire," she answered.

"You'll work for anyone but your own husband and children, eh?" Sir Roger made an effort to sneer, but his lip was puffy where a pellet had glanced off the visor of his helmet. "Go to your tent, I say."

Sir Owain looked shocked. "Those are not words to address a gentlewoman with, sire," he protested.

"One of your plinking roundels were better?" grunted Sir Roger. "Or a whisper, to arrange an assignation?"

Lady Catherine grew quite pale. She took a long breath before words came. Silence fell upon those persons who stood within earshot. "I call God to witness that I am maligned," she said. Her gown streamed with the haste of her stride. As she vanished into her pavilion, I heard the first sob.

Sir Owain stared at the baron with a kind of horror. "Have you lost your senses?" he breathed at last.

Sir Roger hunched thick shoulders, as if to raise a burden. "Not yet. Let my captains of battle meet with me when they've washed and supped. But it might be wisest, Sir Owain, if you would take charge of the camp guard."

The knight bowed again. It was not an insulting gesture, but it reminded us all how Sir Roger had transgressed good manners. He departed and took up his duties briskly. A watch was soon set. Thereafter Sir Owain took Branithar on a walk around the blasted Wersgor camp, to examine that equipment which had been far enough away to remain usable. The blueface had—even during the past few busy days—picked up more English. He talked, lamely but with great earnestness, and Sir Owain listened. I glimpsed this in the last dim twilight, as I hurried to the conference, but could not hear what was being said.

A fire burned high, and torches were stuck in the

ground. The English chieftains sat around the trestle table with alien constellations winking to life overhead. I heard night sough in the forest. All the men were deathly tired, they slumped on the benches, but their eyes never left the baron.

Sir Roger stood up. Bathed, clad in fresh though plain garments, a sapphire ring arrogant on one finger, he betrayed himself only by the dullness of his tone. Though the words were brisk enough, his soul was not in them. I glanced toward the tent where Lady Catherine and his children lay, but darkness hid it.

"Once again," said my lord, "God's grace has aided us to win. In spite of all the destruction we wrought, we've more booty of cars and weapons than we can use. The army that came against us is broken, and only one fortress remains on this entire world!"

Sir Brian scratched his white-bristled chin. "Two can play that game of tossing explosives about," he said. "Dare we remain here? As soon as they recover their wits, they'll find means to fire on us."

"True." Sir Roger's blond head nodded. "That's one reason we must not linger. Another being that it's an uncomfortable dwelling place at best. By all accounts, the castle at Darova is far larger, stronger, and better fitted. Once we've seized it, we need not fear shellfire. And even if Duke Huruga has no means left him whereby to bombard us here, we can be sure he's now swallowed his pride and sent spaceships off to other stars for help. We can look for a Wersgor armada to come against us." He affected not to notice the shudder that went among them, but finished, "For all these reasons, we want Darova for our own, intact."

"To stand off the fleets of a hundred worlds?" cried Captain Bullard. "Nay, now, sire, your pride has curdled and turned to madness. I say, let's get aloft ourselves while we can, and pray God that He will guide us back to Terra."

Sir Roger struck the table with his fist. The noise

cracked across all forest rustlings. "God's wounds!" he roared. "On the day of a victory such as hasn't been known since Richard the Lion Heart, you'd tuck tail between legs and run! I thought you a man!"

Bullard growled deep in his throat, "What did Richard gain in the end, save a ransom payment that ruined his country?" But Sir Brian Fitz-William heard him and muttered low, "I'll hear no treason." Bullard realized what he had said, bit his lip and fell silent. Meanwhile Sir Roger hastened on:

"The arsenals of Darova must have been stripped for the assault on us. Now we have nearly all which remains of their weapons, and we've killed off most of its garrison. Give them time, and they'll rally. They'll summon franklins and yeomen from all over the planet, and march against us. But at this moment, they must be in one hurly-burly. The best they'll be able to do is man the ramparts against us. Counterattack is out of the question."

"So shall we sit outside Darova's walls till their reinforcements come?" gibed a voice in the shadows.

"Better that than sit here, think you not?" Sir Roger's laugh was forced, but a grim chuckle or two responded. And so it was decided.

Our worn-out folk got no sleep. At once they must start their toil, by the brilliant double moonlight. We found several of the great transport aircraft which had been only slightly damaged, being on the fringes of the blast. The artisans among our captives repaired them at spearpoint. Into these we rolled all the weapons and vehicles and other equipment we could. People, prisoners, and cattle followed. Well before midnight, our ships had lumbered into the sky, guarded by a cloud of other vessels with one or two men aboard each. We were none too soon. Hardly an hour after our departure—as we learned later—unmanned flyers loaded with the strongest explosives rained down upon the site of Ganturath.

A cautious pace, through heavens empty of hostile craft, brought us over an inland sea. Miles beyond it, in the middle of a rugged and thickly forested region, we raised Darova. Having been summoned to the control turret to interpret, I saw it in the vision screens, far ahead and far below but magnified to our sight.

We had flown to meet the sun, and dawn glowed pink behind the buildings. These were only ten, low, rounded structures of fused stone, their walls thick enough to withstand almost any blow. They were knitted together with reinforced tunnels. Indeed, nearly all that castle was deep underground, as self-contained as a spaceship. I saw an outer ring of gigantic bombards and missile launchers poke their snouts from sunken emplacements, and the force screen was up, like Satan's parody of a halo. But this seemed mere trimming on the strength of the fortress itself. No aircraft were visible, save our own.

By now I, like most of us, had had some instruction in the use of the far-speaker. I tuned it until the image of a Wersgor officer appeared in its screen. He had obviously been trying to tune in on me, so we had lost several minutes. His face was pale, almost cerulean, and he gulped several times before he could ask: "What do you want?"

Sir Roger scowled. Bloodshot, dark-rimmed eyes, in a face whose flesh seemed melted away by care, gave him a frightful appearance. I having translated, he snapped: "Huruga."

"We . . . we shall not surrender our *grath*. He told us so himself."

"Brother Parvus, tell that idiot I only want to talk to the duke! A parley. Haven't they any idea at all of civilized custom?"

The Wersgor gave us a hurt look, since I told him my lord's exact words, but spoke into a little box and touched a series of buttons. His image was replaced with that of Huruga. The governor rubbed sleep from

his eyes and said with forlorn courage, "Don't expect
to destroy this place as you did the others. Darova
was built to be an ultimate strong point. The heaviest
bombardment could only remove the aboveground
works. If you attempt a direct assault, we can fill the
air and the land with blasts and metal."

Sir Roger nodded. "But how long can you maintain
such a barrage?" he asked mildly.

Huruga bared his sharp teeth. "Longer than you
can mount the assault, you animal!"

"Nonetheless," Sir Roger murmured, "I doubt if
you're equipped for a siege." I could find no Wersgor
term in my limited vocabulary for that last word, and
Huruga seemed to have trouble understanding the cir-
cumlocutions by which I rendered it. When I explained
why it took me so long to translate, Sir Roger nodded
shrewdly.

"I suspected as much," he said. "Look you, Brother
Parvus. These starfaring nations have weapons nigh as
powerful as St. Michael's sword. They can blow up a
city with one shell, and lay waste a shire with ten. But
this being so, how could their battles ever be pro-
longed? Eh? Yon castle is built to take hammer blows.
But a siege? Hardly!"

To the screen: "I shall establish myself near by,
keeping watch on you. At the first sign of life from
your castle, I'll open fire. So 'twere best that your men
stay underground all whiles. At any time you wish to
surrender, call me on the far-speaker, and I'll be
pleased to extend the courtesies of war."

Huruga grinned. I could almost read the thoughts
behind that snout. The English were more than welcome to squat outside, till the avenging armada came!
He blanked the screen.

We found a good camp site well beyond the horizon. It lay in a deep, sheltered valley, through which
a river ran clean and cold and full of fish. Meadows
were dotted throughout the forest; game was abun-

dant, and off duty our men were free to hunt. For a few of those long days, I watched cheer blossom fresh among our people.

Sir Roger gave himself no rest. I think he dared not; for Lady Catherine left her children with their nurse and walked among bowers with Sir Owain. Not untended—they were careful of the proprieties—but her husband would glimpse them and turn to snarl a command at the nearest person.

Hidden away in these woods, our camp was safe enough from shellfire or missiles. Its tents and lean-tos, our weapons and tools, were not a large enough concentration of metal to be sniffed out by one of the Wersgor magnetic devices. Such of our aircraft as maintained watch on Darova, always landed elsewhere. We kept trebuchets loaded, in case any activity were revealed about the fortress; but Huruga was content to wait passive. Sometimes a daring enemy vessel passed overhead, having come from some other spot on the planet. But it never found any target for its explosives, and our own patrol soon forced it away.

Most of our strength—the great ships and guns and war-wagons—were elsewhere all this time. I myself did not see the hunting Sir Roger undertook. I stayed in camp, busying myself with such problems as teaching myself more Wersgor and Branithar more English. I also started classes in the Wersgor language for some of our more intelligent boys. Nor would I have wished to go on the baron's expedition.

He had spacecraft and aircraft. He had bombards to fire both flame and shell. He had a few ponderous turtle-cars, which he hung with shields and pennons and manned with a cavalryman and four men-at-arms each. He went out across the continent and harried.

No isolated estate could withstand his attack. Looting and burning, he left desolation behind him. He killed many Wersgorix, but no more than necessary. The rest he stuffed captive into the huge transport ships. A few times, the franklins and yeomen tried to make a stand. They had hand weapons only; his host scattered them like chaff and chivvied them across their own fields. It took him only a few days and nights to devastate the entire land mass. Then he made a quick foray across an ocean, bombed and flamed whatever he chanced upon, and returned.

To me it seemed a cruel butchery, albeit no worse than this empire had done on many worlds. However, I own I have not always understood the logic of such things. Certainly what Sir Roger did was ordinary European practice in a rebellious province or a hostile foreign country. Yet when he landed in camp again, and his men swaggered forth loaded with jewels and rich fabrics, silver and gold, drunk on stolen liquor and boasting of what they had done, I went to Branithar.

"These new prisoners are beyond my power," I said, "but tell your brothers of Ganturath that before the baron can destroy them, he must take off my own poor head."

The Wersgor gave me a curious look. "What do you care for our sort?" he asked.

"God help me," I replied. "I do not know, save that He must also have made you."

Word of this reached my lord. He summoned me to the tent he now used instead of his pavilion. I saw forest glades choked with captives, milling about like sheep, mumbling and terrified under the English guns. True, their presence was a shield to us. Though the ships' descent must now have revealed our location closely enough to Huruga's magnifiers, Sir Roger had taken care that the governor knew what had happened. But I saw blueskin mothers holding little wailing blue cubs, and it was like a hand about my heart.

The baron sat on a stool, gnawing a haunch of beef. Light and shadow filtered through leaves, checkered his face. "What's this?" he cried. "Are you so fond of yon pigfaces you'll not let me have those we caught at Ganturath?"

I squared my skinny shoulders. "If nothing else, sire," I told him, "think how such a deed must harm your own soul."

"What?" He raised his thick brows. "When was it ever forbidden to set free the captive?"

My turn came to gape. Sir Roger slapped one thigh, guffawing. "We'll keep some few, like Branithar and the artisans, who're useful to us. All the rest we'll herd to Darova. Thousands and thousands. Don't you imagine Huruga's heart will melt with gratitude?"

I stood there in sunlight and tall grass, while "Haw, haw, haw!" bellowed about me.

So under the jeers and spear-prods of our men, that uncounted throng stumbled through beck and brake, until they emerged on cleared land and saw the distant mass of Darova. A few stepped out of the crowd, timorous. The English leaned grinning on their weapons. One Wersgor began to run. No one fired at him. Another broke away, and another. Then the entire swarm of them pelted toward the fortress.

That evening Huruga yielded.

" 'Twas easy enough." Sir Roger chuckled. "I had him bottled up in there. I doubted he had more than just enough supplies, for siegecraft must be a lost art in this country. So, first, I showed him I could lay his whole planet waste—which he'd have to answer for even if we were conquered in the end. Then I gave him all those extra mouths to feed." He slapped my back. When I had been picked up and dusted off, be said, "Well, Brother Parvus, now that we own this world, would you like to head its first abbey?"

Chapter XV

Of course I could not accept any such offer. Quite apart from difficult questions of consecration, I hope I know my humble place in life. Anyhow, at this stage it was mere talk. We had too much else to do, to offer God more than a Mass of thanksgiving.

We let nearly all the recaptured Wersgorix go. On a powerful far-speaker, Sir Roger broadcast a proclamation to Tharixan. He bade every large landholder, in those areas not yet ravaged, to come make submission and take several of the homeless ones back with him. The lesson he had taught was so sharp that for the next few days it swarmed with blue visitors. I must needs deal with them, and forgot what sleep was like. But for the most part they were very meek. Indeed, this race had been supreme among the stars so long that only their soldiers now had occasion to develop a manly contempt for death. Once these had submitted, the burgesses and franklins quickly did likewise—and were so used to having an all-powerful government above them that they never dreamed it might be possible to revolt.

Most of Sir Roger's attention in that period went to training his folk in garrison duty. The castle machines being as simple to operate as most Wersgor equipment, he had soon had women, children, serfs, and aged manning Darova. They should be able to hold it against attack for at least a while. Those who seemed hopelessly incapable in the diabolic arts of meter-reading, button-pushing, and knob-twisting, he put on a safely distant island to care for our livestock.

When transplanted Ansby was thus able to defend itself, the baron gathered his free companions for yet another expedition into the sky. He explained his idea to me beforehand: as yet, I alone had any fluency in the Wersgor tongue, though Branithar (with Father Simon's assistance) was instructing others apace.

"We've done well so far, Brother Parvus," Sir Roger declared. "But alone, we'd never hurl back the Wersgor hosts being raised against us. I hope by now you've mastered their writing and numerology. At least well enough to keep watch on a native navigator and see that he doesn't steer us where we would not go."

"I have studied the principles of their star maps a little, sire," I answered, "though in truth they do not employ charts, but mere columns of figures. Nor do they have mortal steersmen on the spaceships. Rather, they instruct an artificial pilot at the start of the journey, and thereafter the homunculus operates the entire craft."

"How well I know that!" grunted Sir Roger. " 'Twas how Branithar tricked us hither in the first instance. A dangerous wight, that, but too useful to kill. Glad I am not to have him aboard on this voyage; and yet I'm not easy in my heart at leaving him in Darova. . . ."

"But where are you bound, sire?" I interrupted.

"Oh. Aye. That." He knuckled eyes sandy with weariness. "There are other kings than Wersgor. Lesser star-traveling nations, who dread the day when these snoutface fiends will decide to make an end of them. I shall seek allies."

It was an obvious enough move, but I hesitated. "Well?" demanded Sir Roger. "What ails you now?"

"If they have not yet gone to war," I said weakly, "why should the advent of a few backward savages like us make them do so?"

"Hearken, Brother Parvus," said Sir Roger. "I'm weary of this whining about our own ignorance and feebleness. We're not ignorant of the true Faith, are we? Somewhat more to the point, maybe, while the engines of war may change through the centuries, rivalry and intrigue look no subtler out here than at home. Just because we use a different sort of weapons, we aren't savages."

I could scarcely refute his argument, since it was our only hope except for a random flight in search of lost Terra.

The best spaceships were those which had lain in the vaults of Darova. We were outfitting these, when the sun was darkened by a still greater vessel. As it hung up there like a thundercloud, it threw dismay among our folk. But Sir Owain Montbelle came running with a Wersgor engineer in tow, snatched up myself to interpret, and led us to the far-speaker. Standing out of sight of the screen, with sword drawn, Sir Owain made the captive speak with the master of the ship.

It proved to be a merchant craft, paying a regular call at this planet. The sight of Ganturath and Stularax turned into holes horrified its crew. We could easily enough have blasted the ship down, but Sir Owain used his Wersgor puppet to tell the captain there had been a raid from space, beaten off by the Darova garrison, and that he should land here. He obeyed. As the ship's outer portals opened, Sir Owain led a swarm of men aboard and captured it without trouble.

For this, they cheered him night and day. And he made a brave, colorful figure, always prepared to fling a jest or a gallantry. Sir Roger, toiling without pause, grew ever more uncouth. Men stood in awe of him, and some little hatred, since he drove them to such exertions. Sir Owain contrasted, like Oberon versus a bear. Half the women must have been in love with him, though he had songs only for Lady Catherine.

The booty from the giant ship was rich. Best of all, however, were many tons of grain. We tried some of this on our livestock on the island, which was growing thin on the detested blue grass. They accepted the feed as eagerly as if it were English oats. When he heard this, Sir Roger exclaimed, "Whatever planet that comes from is the one we must capture next."

I crossed myself and hurried elsewhere.

But we had little time to lose. It was no secret that Huruga had dispatched spaceships to Wersgorixan immediately after the second battle of Ganturath. They would take a while to reach that distant planet, and the emperor would need a while more to raise a fleet among his widely scattered domains, and thereafter it would take time for the fleet to get back here. But already days had fled from us.

To head the Darova garrison of women, children, aged, and serfs, Sir Roger appointed his wife. I am told that our chroniclers' practice of inventing speeches for the great persons whose lives they write is unscholarly. Yet I knew those two, not just the haughty exterior but (in glimpses, for it was shy) the soul. I can all but see them, in a buried room of the alien castle.

Lady Catherine has hung it with her tapestries, spread rushes on the floor, and left the walls darkened in favor of sconced candles, that this place might seem less eerie to her. She waits in garments of pride, while her husband bids their children farewell. Little Matilda weeps openly. Robert withholds the tears, more or less, until he has closed the door on his father: for he is a de Tourneville.

Slowly, Sir Roger straightens. He has stopped shaving, for lack of time, and the beard curls like wire on his scarred hook-nosed face. The gray eyes look burnt out, and a muscle in his cheek will not stop twitching. Since hot water runs freely here from pipes, he has bathed; but he wears his usual rough old jerkin and patched hose. The baldric of his great sword creaks as he advances toward his wife.

"Well," he says awkwardly, "I must begone."

"Yes." Her back is slender and very straight.

"I believe—" He clears his throat. "I believe you've learned everything needful." When she does not answer: "Remember, 'tis most important to keep those students of the Wersgor tongue hard at their lessons. Otherwise we'll be deaf-mutes among our foes. But never trust our prisoners. Two armed men must always be with each one of them."

"Indeed." She nods. She is uncoifed, and candle-light slides along the coiled auburn hair. "I shall also remember that the pigs don't require that new grain we give the other animals."

"Most important! And be certain to stock this stronghold well. Those of our folk who have eaten native food are still in health, so you can requisition from Wersgor granaries."

Silence thickens about them.

"Well," he says, "I must begone."

"God be with you, my lord."

He stands a moment, studying each smallest tone in her voice. "Catherine—"

"Yes, my lord?"

"I've wronged you," he forces out. "And I've neglected you, what's worse."

Her hands reach out, as if of their own accord. His coarse palms close about them.

"Any man could be mistaken, now and then," she breathes.

He dares look into the blue eyes. "Will you give me a token?" he asks.

"For your safe return—"

He drops hands to her waist, draws her close and cries joyous: "And my final victory! Give me your token, and I'll lay this empire at your feet!"

She pulls herself free. Horror bestrides her lips. "When are you going to start looking for our Earth?"

"What honor is there in slinking home, when we leave the very stars our enemies?" Pride clashes in his words.

"God help me," she whispers, and flees him. He stands a long while, until the sound of her feet has vanished down the cold corridors. Then he turns and walks out to his men.

We could have crowded into one of the big ships but thought it best to disperse ourselves in a score. These had been repainted, using Wersgor supplies, by a lad who possessed some heraldic skill. Now they were scarlet and gold and purple, with the de Tourneville arms and the English leopards emblazoned on the flagship.

Tharixan fell behind us. We went into that strange condition, ducking in and out of more dimensions than Euclid's orderly three, which the Wersgorix called "super-light drive." Again the stars flamed on every hand, and we amused ourselves with naming the new constellations—the Knight, the Plowman, the Arbalest, and more, including some which are not fit to put in this record.

The voyage was not long: a few Earth-days only, as near as we could estimate from the clocks. It rested us, and we were keen as hounds when we coursed into the planetary system of Bodavant.

By now we understood that there are many colors

and sizes of suns, all intermingled. The Wersgorix, like
humans, favored small yellow ones. Bodavant was red-
der and cooler. Only one of its planets was habitable
(the usual case); and while this Boda could have been
settled by men or Wersgorix, they would find it dim
and chilly. Thus our enemies had not troubled to conquer the native Jairs but merely prevented them from
acquiring more colonies than they had when discovered, and forced them into grossly unfavorable trade
agreements.

The planet hung like a huge shield, mottled and
rusty, against the stars, when the native warships
hailed us. We brought our flotilla to an obedient halt.
Rather, we ceased to accelerate, and simply plunged
through space in a hyperbolic sub-light orbit which
the Jair craft matched. But these problems of heavenly
navigation make my poor head ache; I am content to
leave them to the astrologers and the angels.

Sir Roger invited the Jair admiral aboard our flagship. We used the Wersgor language, of course, with
myself as interpreter. But I shall only render the gist
of the conversation, not the tedious byplay which actually took place.

A reception had been prepared, with an eye to
impressing the visitors. The corridor from the portal
to the refectory was lined with warriors. The longbowmen had patched their green doublets and hose,
made their caps gay with feathers, and rested their
dreadful weapons before them. The common men-at-
arms had polished what mail and flat helmets they
owned, and formed an arch of pikes. Beyond, where
the passage grew high and broad enough to allow,
twenty cavalrymen gleamed in full armor of plate, banner and scutcheon, plume and lance, astride our big-
gest chargers. At the final door, Sir Roger's
huntmaster stood with hawk on wrist and a pack of
mastiffs at his feet. Trumpets blared, drums rolled,
horses reared, dogs gave tongue, and as one we made

the ship roar with the deep-throated cry: "God and St. George for merry England! Haro!"

The Jairs looked rather daunted but continued to the refectory. It was hung with the most gorgeous of our looted fabrics. At the end of the long table, Sir Roger, in broidered garments, surrounded by halberdiers and crossbowmen, sat on a throne hastily knocked together by our carpenters. As the Jairs entered, he raised a golden Wersgor beaker and drank their health in English ale. He had wanted to use wine, but Father Simon had decided to reserve it for Holy Communion, pointing out that foreign devils wouldn't know the difference.

"*Wâes hâeil!*" declaimed Sir Roger, an English phrase he loved even when speaking his more usual French.

The Jairs hesitated until page boys showed them to their places with as much ceremony as the royal court. Thereafter I said a rosary and asked a blessing upon our conference. This was not, I confess, done for purely religious reasons. We had already gathered that the Jairs employed certain verbal formulas to invoke hidden powers of body and brain. If they were benighted enough to take my sonorous Latin for a still more impressive version of the same thing, the sin was not ours, was it?

"Welcome, my lord," said Sir Roger. He, too, looked much rested. There was even a sparkle of deviltry about him. Only those who knew him well could have guessed what emptiness housed within. "I pray pardon for my unceremonious entrance into your domain, but the news I bear will scarcely wait."

The Jair admiral leaned tensely forward. He was a little taller than a man, though more slender and graceful, with soft gray fur over his body and a white ruff around his head. The face was cat-whiskered and had enormous purple eyes, but otherwise looked human. That is to say, it looked as human as the faces in a triptych painted by a not very skillful artist. He wore close-fitting garments of brown stuff, with insignia of rank. But drab indeed they looked, he and his eight associates, next to the splendor we had scraped up. His name, we found later, was Beljad sor Van. Our expectation that the one in charge of interplanetary defenses would stand high in the government proved well founded.

"We had no idea the Wersgorix would trust any other folk enough to arm them as allies," he said.

Sir Roger laughed. "Hardly, gentle sir! I am come from Tharixan, which I've just taken over. We're using captured Wersgor ships to eke out our own."

Beljad sat bolt upright. His fur bristled with excitement. "Are you another star-traveling race, then?" he cried.

"We hight Englishmen," Sir Roger evaded. He did not wish to lie to potential allies more than he must, for their indignation on discovering it might prove troublesome. "Our lords have extensive foreign possessions, such as Ulster, Leinster, Normandy—but I'll not weary you with a catalogue of planets." I alone noticed he had not actually said those counties and duchies *were* planets. "To put it briefly, ours is a very old civilization. Our records go back for more than five thousand years." He used the Wersgor equivalent, as nearly as possible. And who shall deny that Holy Writ runs with absolute accuracy from the time of Adam?

Beljad was less impressed than we had expected. "The Wersgorix boast a mere two thousand years of clearly established history, since their civilization rebuilt itself after its final internecine war," he said. "But we Jairs possess a reliable chronology for the past eight millennia."

"How long have you practiced space flight?" Sir Roger asked.

"For about two centuries."

"Ah. Our earliest experiments of that sort were—how long ago, would you say, Brother Parvus?"

"About thirty-five hundred years, at a place called Babel," I told them.

Beljad gulped. Sir Roger continued smoothly, "This universe is so large that the expanding English kingdom did not run into the expanding Wersgor domain until very recently. They didn't realize our true powers but attacked us unprovoked. You know their viciousness. We're a very peaceful race ourselves." We had learned from contemptuous prisoners that the Jair Republic deplored warfare and had never colonized a planet which already had inhabitants. Sir Roger folded his hands and rolled his eyes upward. "Indeed," he said, "one of our most basic commandments is, 'Thou shalt not kill.' Yet it seemed a greater sin, to let so cruel and dangerous a power as Wersgorixan continue to ravage helpless folk."

"Hm." Beljad rubbed his furry brow. "Where does this England of yours lie?"

"Now, now," purred Sir Roger. "You can't expect us to tell even the most honored strangers that, until a better understanding has been reached. The Wersgorix themselves don't know, for we captured their scoutship. This expedition of mine has come hither to punish them and gather information. As I told you, we captured Tharixan with small loss to ourselves. But 'tis not our monarch's way to intervene in affairs that concern other intelligent species, without consulting their wishes. I swear King Edward III has never dreamed of doing so. I'd much prefer to have you Jairs, and others who've suffered at Wersgor hands, join me in a crusade to humble them. And thus you'll earn the right to divide up their empire fairly and squarely with us."

"Are you—the head of a single military force—empowered to undertake such negotiations?" Beljad asked doubtfully.

"Sir, I am no petty noble," the baron answered with great stiffness. "My descent is as lofty as any in your realm. An ancestor of mine, by the name of Noah, was once admiral of the combined fleets of my planet."

"This is so sudden," Beljad faltered. "Unheard of. We cannot—I cannot—it has to be discussed, and—"

"Certes." My lord raised his voice till the chamber rang. "But don't dawdle overly long, gentles. I offer you a chance to help destroy the Wersgor barbarism, whose existence England can no longer suffer. If you'll share the burden of war, you'll share the fruits of conquest. Otherwise we English will be forced to occupy the entire Wersgor domain: for someone must keep order in it. So I say, join the crusade under my leadership, and haro for victory!"

Chapter XVI

The Jairs, like the other free nations, were no simpletons. They invited us to land and be guests on their planet. Strange was that stay, as if we spent it in timeless Elf Hill. I remember slim towers, bridges looped airily between, cities where buildings mingled with parks to make one gigantic pleasance, boats on bright lakes, scholars in robe and veil who would discourse with me of English learning, enormous alchemical laboratories, music that still haunts my dreams. But this is no geographical book. And even the soberest account of ancient non-human civilizations would sound wilder to a common English ear than the fantasies of that notorious Venetian, Marco Polo.

While Jair war leaders, wise men, and politicians sought to probe us for information, however courteously, an expedition hastened to Tharixan to see for itself what had happened. Lady Catherine received them with much pomp and allowed them to interview any Wersgorix they chose. She hid away only Branithar, who would have given too much truth. The rest, even Huruga, had nothing but a confused impression of irresistible onslaught.

Being unfamiliar with the variations in human appearance, they did not realize that the Darova garrison was composed of our weakest. But they counted it and could hardly believe that so small a force as ours had accomplished all this. Surely we must have unknown powers in reserve! When they saw our neatherds, riders on horseback, women cooking over wood fires, they swallowed easily enough an explanation that we English preferred as much open-air simplicity of life as possible; it was an ideal of their own.

Fortunate we were that the language barrier limited them to what they could observe of us with their eyes. Those lads learning Wersgor had, as yet, mastered too few words for intelligible conversation. Many a commoner—or even warrior, it may be—would have blurted his own terror and ignorance, begged them to take him home again, had he been able. As it was, all detailed speech with the English must be filtered through myself. And I relayed Sir Roger's cheerful arrogance.

He did not hide from them that an avenging Wersgor fleet would soon fall on Darova. Rather, he boasted of it. His trap was set, he claimed. If Boda and the other starfaring planets would not help him spring it, he must call England for reinforcements.

The idea of an armada from a totally unknown realm, entering their region of space, disquieted the Jair leaders. I make no doubt that some of them took us for mere adventurers, outlaws perhaps, who could actually count on no help from our birthplace. But then others must have argued:

"Dare we stand by and take no hand in what is to happen? Even if they are pirates, these newcomers have conquered a planet, and show no fear of the whole Wersgor Empire. In every case, we must arm ourselves against the possibility that England is—despite their denials—as aggressive as the blueface nation. So would it not be best to strengthen ourselves by helping this Roger, occupying many planets and taking much booty? The only alternative seems to be to make alliance with Wersgor against him, and that is unthinkable!"

Furthermore, the imagination of the Jair people was captured. They saw Sir Roger and his brilliant companions gallop down their sedate avenues. They heard of the defeat he had inflicted on their old enemies. Their folklore, which had long based itself on the fact that they knew only the smallest portion of the universe, predisposed them to believe that older and stronger races existed beyond their maps. Thus, when they heard that he urged war, they took fire and clamored for it. Boda was a true republic, not a sham one such as the Wersgor had. This popular voice rang loud in the parliament.

The Wersgor ambassador protested. He threatened destruction. But he was far from home, the dispatches he sent would take time to arrive, and meanwhile crowds stoned his residence.

Sir Roger himself conferred with two other emissaries. These were the representatives of the other starfaring nations, Ashenkoghli and Pr?°tans. The odd letters in the latter name are my own, standing respectively for a whistle and a grunt. I will let one such conversation stand for the many that took place.

As usual, it was in the Wersgor language. I had more trouble interpreting than I was wont, since the Pr?°tan was in a box which maintained the heat and poisonous air he needed, and talked through a loudspeaker with an accent worse than my own. I never even tried to know his personal name or rank, for these involved concepts more subtle to the human mind than the books of Maimonides. I thought of him as Tertiary Eggmaster of the Northwest Hive, and privately I named him Ethelbert.

We visitors were seated in a cool blue room, far above the city. While Ethelbert's tentacled shape, dimly seen through glass, labored with formal courtesies, Sir Roger glanced out at the view. "Open windows, broad as a sally port," he muttered. "What an opportunity! How I'd love to attack this place!"

When our talk was begun, Ethelbert said: "I cannot commit the Hives to any policy. I can only send a recommendation. However, since our people have minds less individualistic than average, I may add that my recommendation will carry great weight. At the same time, I am correspondingly hard to convince."

We had already been given to understand this. As for the Ashenkoghli, they were divided into clans; their ambassador here was chief of one and could raise its fleet on his own authority. This so simplified our negotiations that we saw God's purpose revealed. I daresay the confidence we gained thereby was itself a powerful asset to us.

"Surely you, good sir, are aware of the arguments we've given the Jairs," Sir Roger said. "They're no less applicable to Pur—Pur—whatever your by-our-lady planet is called."

I felt an exasperation, that he should throw on me the whole burden of pronunciation and polite rephrasing, and set myself a rosary in penance. Wersgor was so barbarous that I could still not think properly in it. Accordingly, when interpreting Sir Roger's French, I first put the gist into my own boyhood English, then into stately Latin periods, on which firm foundation I could erect a Wersgor structure that Ethelbert mentally translated into Pr?°tan. Marvelous are the works of God.

"The Hives have suffered," admitted the ambassador. "The Wersgorix limit our space fleet and extraplanetary possessions; they exact a heavy tribute of rare metals. However, our home world is useless to them, so we have no fear of ultimate conquest like Boda and Ashenk. Why should we provoke their wrath?"

"I suppose these creatures have no idea of honor," the baron grumbled to me, "so tell him he'll be free of those restrictions and tribute, once Wersgorixan is overthrown."

"Obviously," was the cold reply. "Yet the gain is too small, in comparison with the risk that our planet and its colonies may be bombarded."

"That risk will be much lessened, if all Wersgorixan's foes act together. The enemy'll be kept too busy to take offensive action."

"But no such alliance exists."

"I've reason to believe the Ashenkoghli lord here on Boda plans to join us. Then many other clans of theirs are sure to do likewise, if only to keep him from gaining too much power."

"Sire," I protested in English, "you know that he of Ashenk is less than ready to stake his fleet on this gamble."

"Tell the monster here what I said, anyhow."

"My lord, it isn't true!"

"Ah, but we'll make it come true; so 'tis no lie after all."

I choked on the casuistry but rendered it as required of me. Ethelbert shot back: "What makes you think so? He of Ashenk is known to be a cautious one."

"Certes." It was a shame that the blandness of Sir Roger's tone was wasted on those nonhuman ears. "Therefore he's not about to announce his intention openly. But his staff ... some of 'em blab, or can't resist dropping a hint—"

"This must be investigated!" said Ethelbert. I could all but read his thoughts. He would set his own spies, hireling Jairs, to work.

We hied ourselves elsewhere and resumed some talks Sir Roger had been having with a young Ashenkogh. This fiery centaur was himself eager for a war in which he might win fame and wealth. He explained the details of organization, record-keeping, communication, which Sir Roger needed to know. Then the baron instructed him what documents to forge and leave for Ethelbert's agents to find, what words to let fall in drunkenness, what clumsy attempts to make at bribing Jair officials. . . . Erelong everyone but the Ashenkoghli ambassador himself knew that he was planning to join us.

So Ethelbert sent a recommendation of war to Pr?°t. It went secretly, of course, but Sir Roger bribed the Jair inspector who passed diplomatic messages out in special boxes to the mailships. The inspector was promised an entire archipelago on Tharixan. That was a shrewd investment of my lord's, for it won him the right to show the Ashenkoghli chief that dispatch ere it continued on its way. Since Ethelbert had so much confidence in our cause, the chief sent for his own fleet and wrote letters inviting the lords of allied clans to do likewise.

By now, the military intelligence of Boda knew what was going on. They could certainly not allow Pr?°t and Ashenk to reap so rich a harvest while their planet remained insignificant. Accordingly, they recommended that the Jairs also join the alliance. Thus urged, the parliament declared war on Wersgorixan.

Sir Roger grinned all over his face. " 'Twas easy to do," he said when his captains praised him. "I needed but to inquire the way in which things are done hereabouts, which was never secret. Then the star-folk tumbled into snares which would not have fooled a half-witted prince of Germans."

"But how could that be, sire?" asked Sir Owain. "They're older and stronger and wiser than we."

"The first two, granted," nodded the baron. His

humor was so good that he addressed even this knight with frank fellowship. "But the third, no. Where it comes to intrigue, I'm no master of it myself, no Italian. But the starfolk are like children.

"And why? Well, on Earth there've been many nations and lords for many centuries, all at odds with each other, under a feudal system nigh too complicated to remember. Why've we fought so many wars in France? Because the Duke of Anjou was on the one hand the sovereign king of England and on the other hand a Frenchman! Think you what that led to; and yet 'tis really a minor example. On our Earth, we've perforce learned all the knavery there is to know.

"But up here, for centuries, the Wersgorix have been the only real power. They conquered by only one method, crude obliteration of races which had not weapons to fight back. By sheer force—the accident that they had the largest domain—they imposed their will on the three other nations which possessed such military arts. These, being impotent, never even tried to plot against Wersgorixan. None of this has called for more statecraft or generalship than a snowball fight. It took no skill for me to play on simplicity, greed, dawning fear, and mutual rivalry."

"You are too modest, sire." Sir Owain smiled.

"Argh!" The baron's pleasure vanished. "Satan take such matters. The only important thing now is: here we sit, stewing, until the fleet is raised. And meanwhile the enemy is on his way!"

Indeed, that was a nightmare time. We could not leave Boda to join our women and children in the fortress, for the alliance was still unstable. A hundred times Sir Roger must patch it up, often using means that would cost him dearly in the next life. The rest of us spent our time studying history, languages, geography (or should I say astrology?), and the witchlike mechanic arts. This latter must be done on pretext of comparing local engines with those of our home, to the detriment of the former. Luckily, though not unnaturally—Sir Roger had extracted the information from officers and documents, ere we left Tharixan— certain of the arms we captured there were secret. Thus we could demonstrate an especially effective handgun or explosive ball and claim it was English, taking care that none of our allies got too close a look at it.

The night the Jair liaison ship returned from Thari-xan, with word that the enemy armada had arrived. Sir Roger went alone into his bedchamber. I do not know what happened, but next morning his sword needed sharpening and all the furniture lay in splinters.

God granted, though, that we had not much longer to wait. The Bodavant fleet was already gathered in orbit. Now several dozen lean battlecraft from Ashenk arrived, and soon thereafter the boxlike vessels of Pr?°t lumbered in from their poisonous home world. We embarked and roared off to war.

Our first glimpse of Darova, after we had fought past outlying Wersgor ships and into Tharixan's atmo-sphere, made me doubt that aught was left to rescue. For hundreds of miles around the land lay black, ripped, and desolated. Rock bubbled molten wherever a shell had newly struck. That subtle death which can only be sensed with instruments had lain waste this entire continent, and would linger for years.

But Darova was built to withstand such forces, and Lady Catherine had provisioned it well. I glimpsed a Wersgor flotilla as it screamed low above her force-field. Their missiles burst close, causing the near-solid stone of the aboveground structures to flow on the outside—but leaving the interiors unharmed. The seared earth opened; bombards thrust out like viper tongues, spat lightning, and retracted ere fresh explo-sives could smite. Three Wersgor ships tumbled in ruin. Their wrecks were added to the carnage which was left from an attempt to storm this place on the ground.

Then I saw no more smoke-veiled Darova. For the Wersgorix were upon us in force, and the combat moved up again into space.

Strange was that battle. It was fought at unimaginable distances with fire-beams, cannon shells, unmanned missiles. Ships maneuvered under direction from artificial brains, so fast that only the weight-making fields prevented their crews from being smeared across the bulkheads. Hulls were blown open by near-misses, yet could not sink in airless space: the wounded portions sealed themselves off, and the remainder continued to shoot.

Such was the usual way of space war. Sir Roger made an innovation. It had horrified the Jair admirals when he first proposed it, but he had insisted it was a standard English tactic—which it was, in a way. Actually, of course, he did it for fear that his men would otherwise betray their clumsiness with the hell-weapons.

So he disposed them in numerous small, exceedingly fast craft. Our over-all plan of battle was made highly unorthodox, for no other reason than to maneuver the enemy into certain positions. When that chance came, Sir Roger's boats flitted into the heart of the Wersgor fleet. He lost some few, but the others continued their outrageous orbit, to the very flagship of the foe. It was a monstrous thing, almost a mile long, even big enough to carry force-field generators. But the English used explosives to punch through its hull. Then, in space armor, atop which the knights planted their crests—carrying sword, ax, halberd, and bow, as well as handguns—they boarded.

They were not enough to seize that entire labyrinth of corridors and cabins. Yet they enjoyed themselves, suffered small loss (sailors out here being untrained in hand-to-hand fighting), and threw matters into a confusion which vastly aided our general assault. Eventually the crew abandoned that ship. Sir Roger saw them doing so and withdrew his own troop just before the hull was blown to bits.

Only God and the more warlike saints know if his action proved decisive. The allied fleet was outnumbered and very much out-gunned, so every gain we made was valuable out of proportion. On the other hand, our attack had come as a surprise. And we had boxed the foe between ourselves and Darova, whose largest missiles flew into space itself to destroy Wersgor craft.

I cannot describe the vision of St. George, for it was not my privilege to observe this. However, many a sober, trustworthy man-at-arms swore that he saw the holy knight ride down the Milky Way in a foam of stars and impale enemy ships on his lance like so many dragons. Be this as it may, after many hours which I remember but dimly, the Wersgonix gave up. They withdrew in good order, having lost perhaps a fourth of their fleet, and we did not pursue them far.

Instead, we hovered above blackened Darova. Sir Roger and the chiefs of his allies went down in a boat. In the central underground hall, the English garrison, grimy and exhausted from days of battle, gave a feeble cheer. Lady Catherine took time to bathe and garb herself in her best, for honor's sake. She swept out like a queen to greet the captains.

But when she saw her husband, standing in dinted space armor against the chilly glow-light, her stride faltered. "My lord—"

He took off his glazed helmet. The air tubes got somewhat in the way of his knightly gesture, as he tucked it under an arm and went to one knee before her. "No," he cried aloud. "Say not that. Let me rather say, 'My lady and love.'"

She advanced like a sleepwalker. "Is the victory yours?"

"No. Yours."

"And now—"

He rose, grimacing as the necessities clamped back down on him. "Conferences." he said. "Repair of battle damage. Making of new ships, raising of more armies. Intrigues among allies, heads to knock together, laggards to hearten. And fighting to do, always fighting. Until, God willing, the bluefaces are whipped back to their home planet and submit—" He stopped. Her face had lost its quick lovely color. "But for tonight, my lady," he said, unskillfully, though he must have rehearsed it many times, "I think we've earned the right to be alone, that I may praise you."

She drew a shaken breath. "Did Sir Owain Montbelle live?" she asked. When he did not say no, she crossed herself, and a tiny smile flickered on her lips. Then she bade the alien captains welcome and held out her hand for them to kiss.

Chapter XVII

I come now to a grievous part of this history, and the most difficult to write. Nor was I present, save at the very end.

This was because Sir Roger hurled himself into his crusade as if he fled from something—which in a way was true—and I was dragged with him like a leaf whirled along in a gale. I was his interpreter, but at every moment when we had naught else to do I became his teacher and would instruct him in Wersgor until my poor weak flesh could endure no more. My last glimpse, ere I toppled into sleep, would be of candlelight guttering on my lord's haggard face. Then he would often as not summon a doctor of the Jair language, who would teach him until dawn. At this rate, it was not many weeks before he could curse hideously in both tongues.

Meanwhile, he drove his allies nigh as hard as he did himself. The Wersgorix must be given no chance to recover. Planet after planet must be attacked, reduced, and garrisoned, so that the foe always fought off balance, on the defensive. In this task, we had much help from enslaved native populations. As a rule, these need only be given arms and leadership. Then they attacked their masters in such hordes, with such ferocity, that the latter fled to us for protection. Jairs, Ashenkoghli, and Pr?°tans were horrified. They had no experience in such matters; whereas Sir Roger had encountered the Jacquerie in France. In their bewilderment, his fellow chieftains came more and more to accept his unquestioned leadership.

The ins and outs of what happened are too complex, too various from world to world, for this paltry record. But in essence, on each inhabited planet, the Wersgorix had destroyed whatever original civilization existed. Now the Wersgor system in turn was toppled. Into this vacuum—unreligion, anarchy, banditry, famine, the ever-present menace of a blueface return, the necessity of training the natives themselves to eke out our thin garrisons—Sir Roger stepped. He had a solution to these problems, one hammered out in Europe during those not dissimilar centuries after Rome fell: the feudal system.

But just when he was thus laying the cornerstone of victory, it crumbled for him. God rest his soul! No more gallant knight ever lived. Even now, a lifetime later, tears dim my old eyes, and I were fain to hurry over this part of the chronicle. Since I witnessed so little, it would be excusable for me to do so.

However, those who betrayed their lord did not rush into it. They stumbled. Had Sir Roger not been blind to all warning signs, it would never have happened. Therefore I shall not set it down in cold words, but fall back on the earlier (and, I think, truer) practice of inventing whole scenes, that folk now dust may live again and be known, not as abstract villainies, but as fallible souls: on whom perhaps God, at the very last, had mercy.

We begin on Tharixan. The fleet had just departed to seize the first Wersgor colony of its long campaign. A Jair garrison occupied Darova. But those English women, children, and grandsires who had so valiantly held fast, were given what reward lay in Sir Roger's power. He moved them to that island where our kine were pastured. There they could dwell in woods and fields, erecting houses, herding, hunting, sowing and reaping, almost as if it were home. Lady Catherine was set to rule over them. She kept Branithar, of the Wersgor captives, as much to prevent his revealing too much to the Jairs as to continue giving instruction in his language. She also had a small fast spaceship for emergency use. Visits from the Jairs across the sea were discouraged, lest they observe too closely.

It was a peaceful time, save in my lady's heart.

For her the great grief began the day after Sir Roger embarked. She walked across a flowery meadow, hearing wind sough in the trees. A pair of her maids followed behind. Through the woods came voices, the ring of an ax, the bark of a dog, but to her they seemed of dreamlike remoteness.

Suddenly she halted. For a moment she could only stare. Then one hand stole to the crucifix on her breast. "Mary, have pity." Her maids, well-trained, slipped back out of earshot.

Sir Owain Montbelle hobbled from the glade. He was in his gayest garb, nothing but a sword to remind her of war. The crutch on which he leaned hardly interfered with his gracefulness as he swept off his plumed bonnet in a bow.

"Ah," he cried, "this instant the place has become Arcady, and old Hob the swineherd whom I just met is heathen Apollo, harping a hymn to the great witch Venus."

"What's this?" Catherine's eyes were blue dismay. "Has the fleet returned?"

"Nay." Sir Owain shrugged. "Blame my own awkwardness yestre'en. I was frolicking about, playing ball, when I stumbled. My ankle twisted, and remains so weak and tender that I'd be useless in battle. Perforce I deputed my command to young Hugh Thorne and flitted hither in an aircraft. Now I must wait till I am healed, then borrow a ship and a Jair pilot to rejoin my comrades."

Catherine tried desperately to speak sober words. "In . . . in his language lessons . . . Branithar has mentioned that the star folk have s-s-strange chirurgic arts." She flushed like fire. "Their lenses can look . . . even inside a living body . . . and they inject simples which heal the worst wound in days."

"I thought of that," said Sir Owain. "For of course I would not be a laggard in war. But then I remembered my lord's strict orders, that our entire hope depends for the nonce on convincing these demon races we are as learned as they."

She clasped the crucifix still tighter.

"So I dared not ask help of their physicians," he continued. "I told them instead that I remain behind to attend certain matters of moment, and carry this crutch as a penance for sin. When nature has healed me, I will depart. Though in truth, 'twill be like tearing out my own heart, to go from you."

"Does Sir Roger know?"

He nodded. They passed hastily to something else. That nod was a black lie. Sir Roger did not know. None of his men dared tell him. I might have ventured it, for he would not strike a man of the cloth, but I was also ignorant. Since the baron avoided Sir Owain's company these days, and had enough else to occupy his mind, he never thought of it. I suppose in his inmost soul he did not want to think of it.

Whether Sir Owain really hurt his ankle, I dare not say. But it would be a strange coincidence. However, I doubt if he had planned his final treason in detail.

Most likely his wish was to continue certain talks with Branithar and see what developed.

He leaned close to Catherine. His laughter rang out. "Until I go," he said, "I feel free to bless the accident."

She looked away, and trembled. "Why?"

"I think you know." He took her hand.

She withdrew it. "I beg you, remember my husband is at war."

"Misdoubt me not!" he exclaimed. "I would sooner lie dead than be dishonored in your eyes."

"I could never ... misdoubt ... so courteous a knight."

"Is that all I am? Courteous only? Amusing? A jester for your weary moments? Well-a-day, better Catherine's fool than Venus' lover. So let me then entertain you." And he lifted his clear voice in a roundel to her praise.

"No—" She moved from him, like a doe edging clear of the hunter. "I am ... I gave pledges—"

"In the courts of Love," he said, "there is only one pledge, Love itself." The sunlight burnished his hair.

"I have two children to think of," she begged.

He grew somber. "Indeed, my lady. I've often dandled Robert and little Matilda on my knee. I hope I may do it again, while God allows."

She faced him afresh, almost crouching. "What do you mean?"

"Oh—Nay." He looked into the murmurous woods, whose leaves were of no shape or color ever seen on Earth. "I would not voice disloyalty."

"But the children!" This time it was she who seized his hand. "In Christ's holy name, Owain, if you know aught, speak!"

He kept his face turned from her. He had a fine profile. "I am not privy to any secrets, Catherine," he said. "Belike you can judge the question better than I. For you know the baron best."

"Does anyone know him?" she asked in bitterness.

He said, very low, "It seems to me that his dreams grow with each new turn of fate. At first he was content to fly to France and join the King. Then he would liberate the Holy Land. Brought here by evil fortune, he responded nobly: none can deny that. But having gained a respite. has he sought Terra again? No, he took this whole world. Now he is off to conquer suns. Where will it end?"

"Where—" She could not continue. Nor could she pull her gaze from Sir Owain.

The knight said, "God puts bounds to all things. Unlimited ambition is the egg of Satan, from which only woe can hatch. Does it not seem to you, my lady, when you lie sleepless at night, that we will overreach ourselves and be ruined?"

After a long while he added: "Wherefore I say, Christ and His Mother help all the little children."

"What can we do?" she cried in her anguish. "We've lost our way to Earth!"

"It might be found again," he said.

"In a hundred years of search?"

He watched her in silence for a while before he answered:

"I would not raise false hopes in so sweet a bosom. But from time to time I've conversed a little with Branithar. Our knowledge of each other's tongues is but scant, and certes he does not trust any human overmuch. Yet . . . a few things he has said . . . make me think that perhaps the road home might be found."

"What?" Both her frantic hands seized him. "How? Where? Owain, are you gone mad?"

"No." he said with studied roughness. "But let us suppose this be true, than Branithar can guide us despite all. He'll not do so without a price, I suppose. Do you think Sir Roger would renounce his crusade and go quietly back to England?"

"He—why—"

"Has he not said again and yet again: while the Wersgor power remains, England lies in mortal danger? Would not the rediscovery of Terra only lead him to redouble his efforts? Nay, what use is it to learn our way back? The war would still continue, until it ended in our destruction."

She shuddered and crossed herself.

"Since I am here," Sir Owain finished, "I may as well try to learn if the homeward route can indeed be found. Perhaps you can think of some means to use that knowledge, ere it is too late."

He bade her a courtly good day, which she did not hear, and limped on into the forest.

Chapter XVIII

Many long Tharixanian days passed: weeks of Earth time. Having taken the first planet he aimed at, Sir Roger went on to the next. Here, while his allies distracted the enemy gunners, he stormed the main castle afoot, using foliage to conceal his approach. This was the place where Red John Hameward actually did rescue a captive princess. True, she had green hair and feathery antennae, nor was there any possibility of issue between her species and our own. But the humanlikeness, and exceeding gratitude, of the Vashtunari—who had just been in process of being conquered—did much to cheer lonely Englishmen. Whether or not the prohibitions of Leviticus are applicable is still being hotly debated.

The Wersgorix counterattacked from space, basing their fleet in a ring of planetoids. Sir Roger had taken an opportunity while en route to turn off the artificial weight aboard ship and let his men practice movement under such conditions. So now, armored against vacuum, our bowmen made that famous raid called the Battle of the Meteors. Cloth-yard shafts pierced many a Wersgor spacesuit without fire-flash or magnetic force-pulse to give away a man's position. With their base thus depleted of manpower, the enemy withdrew from the entire system. Admiral Beljad had grabbed off three other suns while they were occupied with this one, so their new retreat was a long one.

And on Tharixan, Sir Owain Montbelle made himself pleasant to Lady Catherine. And he and Branithar felt each other out, cautiously, under pretext of language study. At last they thought they had touched mutual understanding.

It remained to convince the baroness.

I believe both moons had risen. Treetops were hoar with that radiance; double shadows reached across grass where dew glittered; by now, the night sounds had become familiar and peaceful. Lady Catherine left her pavilion, as often after her children were fallen asleep and she unable to. Wrapped in a hooded mantle, she walked down a lane intended for the street of the new village, past half-finished wattle huts that were blocks of shadow under the moons, and out onto a meadow through which ran a brook. The water flowed and sparkled with light; it chimed on rocks. She drank a warm strange smell of flowers, and remembered English hawthorn when they crowned the May Queen. She remembered standing on the pebble beach at Dover, newly wed, when her husband had embarked on a summer's campaign, and waving and waving until the last sail was vanished. Now the stars were a colder shore, and no one would see her kerchief if it fluttered. She bent her head and told herself she would not weep.

Harp strings jingled in the dark. Sir Owain trod forth. He had discarded his crutch, though he still affected a limp. A massy silver chain caught moonlight across his black velvet tunic, and she saw him smile.

"Oho," he said softly, "the nymphs and dryads are out!"

"Nay." Despite all resolutions, she felt gladdened. His banter and flattery had lightened so many sad hours; they brought back her courtly girlhood. She fluttered protesting hands, knew she was being coy, but could not stop. "Nay, good knight, this is unseemly."

"Beneath such a sky, and in such a presence, nothing is unseemly," he told her. "For we are assured there is no sin in Paradise."

"Speak not so!" Her pain came back redoubled. "If we have wandered anywhere, 'tis into hell."

"Wherever my lady is, there is Paradise."

"Is this any place to hold a Court of Love?" she gibed bitterly.

"No." He grew solemn in his turn. "Indeed, a tent—or a log cabin, when they complete it—is no place for her to dwell who commands all hearts. Nor are these marches a fit home for you . . . or your children. You should sit among roses as Queen of Love and Beauty, with a thousand knights breaking lances in your honor and a thousand minstrels singing your charms."

She tried to protest, " 'Twould be enough to see England again—" but her voice would go no further—

He stood gazing into the brook where twin moonpaths glided and shivered. At last he reached beneath his cloak. She saw steel gleam in his hand. An instant she shrank away. But he raised the crosshilt upward and said, in those rich tones he well knew how to use: "By this token of my Saviour and my honor, I swear you shall have your wish!"

His blade sank. He stared at it. She could scarcely hear him when he added, "If you truly wish it."

"What do you mean?" She drew her mantle tight, as if the air were cold. Sir Owain's gaiety was not the hoarse boisterousness of Sir Roger, and his present gravity was more eloquent than her husband's stammering protestations. Yet briefly she felt afraid of Sir Owain, and would have given all her jewels to see the baron clank from the forest.

"You never say plainly what you mean," she whispered.

He turned a face of disarming boyish ruefulness on her. "Mayhap I never learned the difficult art of blunt speech. But if now I hesitate, 'tis because I am loath to tell my lady that which is hard."

She straightened. For a moment, in the unreal light, she looked strangely like Sir Roger; it was his gesture. Then she was only Catherine, who said with forlorn courage, "Tell me anyhow."

"Branithar can find Terra again," he said.

She was not one to faint. But the stars wavered. She regained awareness leaning against Sir Owain's breast. His arms enclosed her waist, and his lips moved along her cheek toward her mouth. She drew a little away, and he did not pursue his kiss. But she felt too weak to leave his embrace.

"I call this hard news," he said, "for reasons I've discussed erenow. Sir Roger will not give up his war."

"But he could send _us_ home!" she gasped.

Sir Owain looked bleak. "Think you he will? He needs every human soul to maintain his garrisons and keep up an appearance of strength. You recall what he proclaimed ere the fleet left Tharixan. As soon as a planet seems strongly enough held, he will send off people of this village to join those few men he has newly created dukes and knights. As for himself—oh, aye, he talks of ending England's peril, but has he never spoken of making you a queen?"

She could only sigh, remembering a few words let slip.

"Branithar himself shall explain." Sir Owain whistled.

The Wersgor stepped from a canebrake where he had waited. He could move about freely enough, since he had no hope of escaping the island. His stocky form was well clad in plundered raiment, which glittered as with a thousand tiny pearls. The round, hairless, long-eared, snouted face no longer seemed ugly; the yellow eyes were even gay. By now Catherine could follow his language well enough for him to address her.

"My lady will wonder how I could ever find my way back along a zigzag route taken through swarming uncharted stars," he said. "When the navigator's notes were lost at Ganturath, I myself despaired. So many suns, even of the type of your own, lie within the radius of our cruise, that random search might require a thousand years. This is the more true since nebulosities in space hide numbers of stars until one chances fairly close to them. To be sure, if any deck officers of my ship had survived, they could have narrowed down the search somewhat. But my own work was with the engines. I saw stars only in casual glimpses, and they meant nothing to me. When I tricked your people—rue the day!—all I did was push an emergency control which instructed an automaton to pilot us hither."

A lift of excitement brought back impatience to Catherine. She pulled free of Sir Owain's arms and snapped, "I'm not altogether a fool. My lord respected me enough to try to explain these things to me, however ill I listened. What news have you discovered?"

"Not discovered," said Branithar. "Remembered. 'Tis an idea which should have occurred to me erenow, but there was so much happening— Well . . .

"Know, then, my lady, that there are certain beacon stars, brilliant enough to be visible throughout the spiral arm of the Via Galactica. They are used in navigation. Thus, if the suns called (by us) Ulovarna, Yariz, and Gratch, are seen to form a certain configuration with respect to each other, one must be in a certain region of space. Even a crude visual estimate of the angles would fix one's position within twenty or so light-years. This is not too large a sphere to find a given yellow-dwarf sun like your own."

She nodded, slowly and thoughtfully. "Aye. Belike you think of bright stars like Sirius and Rigel. . . ."

"The major stars in the sky of a planet may not be the ones I mean," he warned. "They may simply happen to lie close by. Actually, a navigator would need a good sketch of your constellations, with numerous bright stars indicated by color (as seen from airless space). Given enough data, he could analyze and determine which *must* be the beacon giants. Then their relative positions would tell him where they had been observed from."

"I think I could draw the Zodiac for you," said Lady Catherine uncertainly.

"It would be of no use, mistress," Branithar told her. "You have no skill in identifying stellar types by eye. I admit I have little enough: no training at all, merely the casual hearsay about other people's special crafts which one picks up. And while I did chance to be in the control turret once, while our ship was orbiting about Terra making long-range observations, I paid no special heed to the constellations. I have no memory of what they looked like."

Her heart tumbled downward. "But then we're still lost!"

"Not quite so. I should say, I have no conscious memory. Yet we Wersgorix have long known that the mind is composed of more than the self-aware portion."

"True," agreed Catherine wisely. "There is the soul."

"Er . . . that's not exactly what I meant. There is an unconscious or half-conscious depth in the mind, the source of dreams and— Well, anyhow, let it suffice that this unawareness never forgets. It records even the most trivial things which ever impinged on the senses. If I were thrown into a trance and given proper guidance, I could draw quite an accurate picture of the Terrestrial sky, as glimpsed by myself.

"Then a skilled navigator, his star tables at hand, could winnow this crop with his arts mathematic. It would require time. Many blue stars might be Gratch, for example, and only detailed study could eliminate those which are in an impossible relationship to (shall we say) the globular cluster assumed to be Torgelta. Eventually, however, he would narrow the possibilities down to that smallish region whereof I spoke. Then he could flit thither, with a space pilot to aid him, and they could visit all yellow-dwarf stars in the neighborhood until they found Sol."

Catherine smote her hands together. "But this is wonderful!" she cried. "Oh, Branithar, what reward do you wish? My lord will bestow a kingdom on you!"

He planted his thick legs wide, looked up into her shadowed face and said with the surly valor we had come to know:

"What joy would a kingdom give me, built from the shards of my people's empire? Why should I help find your England again, if it only brings more Englishmen ravening hither?"

She clenched her fists and said with Norman bleakness, "You'll not withold your knowledge from One-Eyed Hubert."

He shrugged. "The unaware mind is not readily evoked, my lady. Your barbarous tortures might set up an impassable barrier." He reached beneath his tunic. Suddenly a knife gleamed in his hand. "Not that I would endure them. Stand back! Owain gave me this. I know well enough where my own heart lies."

Catherine whirled about with a tiny shriek.

The knight laid both hands on her shoulders. "Hear me before you judge," he said swiftly. "For weeks I've been trying to sound out Branithar. He dropped hints. I dropped hints in turn. We bargained like two Saracen merchants, never openly admitting that we bargained. At last he named that dagger as the price of spreading out his wares for me to see. I could not imagine him harming any of us with it. Even our children now go about with better weapons than a knife. I took it on myself to agree. Then he told me what he has now told you."

The tautness shuddered out of her. She had taken too many shocks in all this time, with too much fear and solitude in between. Her strength was drained.

"What do you require?" she asked.

Branithar ran a thumb along his knife blade, nodded, and sheathed it again. He spoke quite gently. "First, you must obtain a good Wersgor mind-physician. I can find one with the help of this planet's Domesday Book, which is kept at Darova. You can borrow it from the Jairs on some pretext. This physician has to work together with a skilled Wersgor navigator, who can tell him what questions to ask of me and guide my pencil as I draw the map in my trance. Later we will also need a space pilot; and I insist on a pair of gunners as well. These can also be found somewhere on Tharixan. You can tell your allies you want them to help search out technical secrets of the enemy."

"When you have your star map, what?"

"Well, I shall not turn it freely over to your husband! I suggest that we go secretly aboard your spaceship. There will be a fair balance of power: you humans holding the weapons, we Wersgorix the knowledge. We will stand ready to destroy those notes, and ourselves, if you betray us. At long range, we can haggle with Sir Roger. Your own pleas ought to sway him. If he withdraws from the war, transportation home can be arranged, and our nation will undertake to leave yours alone hereafter."

"If he won't agree?" Her voice remained dull.

Sir Owain leaned close, to whisper in French: "Then you and the children ... and myself ... will nonetheless be returned. But Sir Roger must not be told this, of course."

"I cannot think." She covered her face. "Father in Heaven, I know not what to do!"

"If your folk persist in this lunatic war," Branithar said, "it can only end in their destruction."

Sir Owain had told her the same thing, over and over, all this time when he was the only one of her station on this planet, the only one to whom she could freely talk. She remembered scorched corpses in the fortress ruins; she thought how small Matilda had screamed during the siege of Darova, each time a shellburst rocked the walls; she thought of green English woods where she had gone hawking with her lord in the first years of their marriage, and of the years he now expected to spend fighting for a goal she could not understand. She lifted her face to the moons, light ran cold along her tears, and she said, "Yes."

Chapter XIX

I cannot tell what drove Sir Owain to his treachery. Two souls had ever striven in his breast; his deepest heart must always have remembered how his mother's people had suffered at the hands of his father's. In part, no doubt, his feelings were truly what he claimed to Catherine: horror at the situation, doubt of our victory, love for her person, and concern for her safety. And in part there was a less honorable motive, which may have begun as an idle thought but waxed with time—what might not be done on Terra with a few Wersgor weapons! Reader of my chronicle, when you pray for the souls of Sir Roger and Lady Catherine, say a little word for unhappy Sir Owain Montbelle.

Whatever took place in his secret self, the recreant acted with outward boldness and intelligence. He kept close watch upon the Wersgorix gotten to assist Branithar. During the weeks of their toil, while that which Branithar had forgotten was extracted from his dreams and studied with mathematic devices of more than

Arabian cunning, the knight quietly prepared the spaceship to go. And always he must keep up the heart of his fellow conspirator, the baroness.

She wavered in her resolve, wept, stormed, yelled at him to depart her presence. Once a vessel arrived with orders for so-and-so many people to come settle on yet another captured planet. Aboard it was a letter which Sir Roger had sent his wife. He dictated this to me, for his spelling was not always under control, and I took it on myself to polish his phrases a little, so that through their stiffness might come some hint of a humble and enduring love. Catherine at once wrote a reply, admitting her actions and imploring forgiveness. But Sir Owain anticipated this, got the letter ere the ship departed again, burned it, and persuaded her to abide by their scheme. It was, he swore, the best for all concerned, even for her lord.

Finally she gave her dwindled village some excuse about joining her husband. She embarked with the children and two maid-servants. Sir Owain had learned enough space arts to send the ship to some known, clear destination—a mere matter of pressing the correct buttons—so he could also join them openly. The night before, he had smuggled the Wersgorix aboard: Branithar, the physician, the pilot, the navigator, and a couple of soldiers trained to use those bombards projecting out of the hull.

Those were useless within the ship, where Owain and Catherine bore the only guns. Extra hand weapons were stowed in the clothes chest in her bedchamber, and one maid was always stationed there. The girls were so terrified of the bluefaces that had any attempted to come take a gun, the screaming would have brought Sir Owain in haste.

Nonetheless, knight and lady must watch their associates like wolves. For the obvious thing for Branithar to do was steer to Wersgorixan itself, where he could inform the emperor of Terra's location. With all

England a hostage, Sir Roger must submit. Even the knowledge that we were not from a great space-traveling civilization, but simple and innocent Christian folk, mere lambs led to this slaughter, would have so heartened the Wersgorix and demoralized our allies, that Branithar must on no account be allowed to communicate the secret.

Not until Sir Owain's plans had reached fruition. Perhaps never. I am sure Branithar himself foresaw a certain awkwardness at the moment when he had deposited his human comrade on English soil. No doubt he made his own devious plans against it. But for the present, their interests ran in the same channel.

These considerations alone will disprove certain sniggering canards about Lady Catherine. She and Sir Owain dared never be at ease simultaneously. They must stand watch on watch, gun at hip, the entire voyage, lest their crew overwhelm them. It was the most effective chaperonage in history. Not that she would have misbehaved in any event. Confused and frightened she might become, but she was never faithless.

Sir Owain felt reasonably confident that Branithar's data were honest. But he insisted on proof. The boat flew for some ten days, to the indicated region of space. Another couple of weeks were spent casting about, examining various hopeful stars. I shall not try to chronicle what the humans felt, as constellations gradually became familiar again; nor that single aerial glimpse which their bargain with distrustful Branithar vouchsafed them, when Dover castle fluttered its pennons above white cliffs. I do not believe they ever spoke about it.

Their ship screamed from atmosphere and lined out again for the hostile stars.

Chapter XX

Sir Roger had established himself on the planet we named New Avalon. Our folk needed a rest, and he needed time to settle many questions of securing that vast kingdom which had already fallen to him. He was furthermore in secret negotiation with the Wersgor governor of an entire star cluster. This person seemed willing to yield up all he controlled, could we give him suitable bribes and guarantees. The haggling went slowly, but Sir Roger felt confident of its outcome.

"They know so little about the detection and use of traitors out here," he remarked to me, "that I can buy this fellow for less than an Italian city. Our allies never attempted this, for they imagined that the Wersgor nation must be as solid as their own. Yet isn't it logic, that so great a sprawl of estates, separated by days and weeks of travel, must in many ways resemble a European country? Though even more corruptible—"

"Since they lack the true Faith," I said.

"Hm, well, yes, no doubt. Though I've never found

Christians who refused a bribe on religious grounds. I was thinking that the Wersgor type of government commands no fealty."

At any rate, we had a little while of peace, camped in a dale beneath dizzyingly tall cliffs. A waterfall rushed arrow-straight into a lake more clear than glass, ringed with trees. Even our sprawling, brawling English camp could not hurt so much beauty.

I had settled down outside my own little tent, at ease in a rustic chair. My hard studies laid aside for a moment, I indulged myself with a book from home, a relaxing chronicle of the miracles of St. Cosmas. As if from far off, I heard the crackle of fire-gun practice, the *zap* of archery, the cheerful clatter of quarterstaff play. I was almost asleep, when feet thudded to a halt beside me.

Startled, I blinked upward at the terrified face of a baronial esquire. "Brother Parvus!" he said. "In God's name, come at once!"

"Ugh, uh, whoof?" I said in my drowsiness.

"Exactly," he groaned.

I gathered my cassock and trotted at his heels. Sunlight and blossoming bowers and birdsong overhead were suddenly remote. I knew only the leap of my heart and the realization of how few and weak and far from home we were. "What's awry?"

"I know not," said the esquire. "A message came on the far-speaker, relayed from space by one of our patrol ships. Sir Owain Montbelle desired private talk with my lord. I know not what was spoken on the narrow beam. But Sir Roger came staggering out like a blind man and roared for you. Oh, Brother Parvus, it was horrible to see!"

I thought that I should pray for us all, doomed if the baron's strength and cunning could no longer uphold us. But I was at once too full of pity for him alone. He had borne too much, too long, with never a soul to share the burden. All brave saints, I thought, stand by him now.

Red John Hameward mounted guard outside the portable Jair shelter. He had spied his master's strickenness, and dashed thither from the target range. With strung bow, he bellowed at the crowd that milled and muttered: "Get you back! Back to your places! God's death, I'll put this arrow through the first by-our-lady sod to pester my lord, and break the by-our-lady neck o' the next! Go, I say!"

I brushed the giant aside and entered. It was hot within the shelter. Sunlight filtered through its translucency had a thick color. Mostly it was furnished with homely things. leather, tapestry, armor. But one shelf held instruments of alien manufacture, and a large far-speaker set was placed on the floor.

Sir Roger slumped in a chair before this, chin on breast, his big hands hanging limp. I stole up behind him and laid my own hand on his shoulder. "What is the matter, sire?" I asked, as softly as might be.

He hardly moved. "Go away," he said.

"You called for me."

"I knew not what I was doing. This is between myself and— Go away."

His voice was flat, but it took my whole small stock of courage to walk around in front of him and say, "I presume your receiver inscribed the message as usual?"

"Aye. No doubt. I'd best wipe out that record."

"No."

His gray gaze lifted toward me. I remembered a wolf I had once seen trapped, when the townsfolk closed in to make an end of it. "I don't want to harm you, Brother Parvus," he said.

"Then don't," I answered brusquely, and stooped to turn on the playback.

He gathered his powers, in great weariness. "If you

see that message," he warned, "I must kill you for my honor."

I thought back to my boyhood. There had been various short, pungent, purely English words in common use. I selected one and pronounced it. From the corner of an eye, as I squatted by the dials, I saw his jaw fall. He sank back into his chair. I pronounced another English word for good measure.

"Your honor lies in the well-being of your people," I added. "You're not fit to judge anything which can so shake you as this. Sit down and let me hear it."

He huddled into himself. I turned a switch. Sir Owain's face leaped into the screen. I saw that he was also gaunt, the handsomeness less evident, the eyes dry and burning. He spoke in formal, courteous wise, but could not hide his exultation.

I cannot remember his exact words. Nor do they matter. He told his lord what had happened. He was now in space, with the stolen ship. He had approached close to New Avalon to beam this call but taken to his heels again immediately it was spoken. There was no hope of finding him in that vastness. If we yielded, he said, he would arrange the transportation home of our folk, and Branithar assured him the Wersgor emperor would promise to keep hands off Terra. If we did not yield, the recreant would go to Wersgorixan and reveal the truth about us. Then, if necessary, the foe could recruit enough French or Saracen mercenaries to destroy us; but probably the demoralization of our allies, as they learned our weakness, would suffice to bring them to terms. In either case, Sir Roger would never see his wife and children again.

Lady Catherine entered the screen. I recall her words. But I do not choose to write them down. When the record was ended, I wiped it out myself.

We were silent awhile, my lord and I.

At last: "Well," he said, like an old man.

I stared at my feet. "Montbelle said they would re-enter communication range at a certain hour tomorrow, to hear your decision," I mumbled. " 'Twould be possible to send numerous unmanned ships, loaded with explosive fused by a magnetic nose, along that far-speaker beam. Belike he could be destroyed."

"You've already asked much of me, Brother Parvus," said Sir Roger. Still his words had no life in them. "Ask me not to slay my lady and children . . . unshriven."

"Aye. Ah, could the vessel be captured? No," I answered myself. " 'Twould be a practical impossibility. Any single shot which struck close enough to a little ship like that would more likely make dust of it than merely disable its engines. Or else the damage would be small, and he would at once flee faster than light."

The baron raised his congealed face. "Whatever happens," he said, "no one is to know my lady's part in this. D'you understand? She's not in her right mind. Some fiend has possessed her."

I regarded him with a pity still greater than before. "You're too brave to hide behind such foolishness," I said.

"Well, what can I do?" he growled.

"You can fight on—"

"Hopelessly, once Montbelle has gone to Wersgorixan."

"Or you can accept the terms offered."

"Ha! How long d' you think the blueskins would actually leave Terra in peace?"

"Sir Owain must have some reason to believe they will," I said cautiously.

"He's a fool." Sir Roger's fist smote the arm of the chair. He sat up straight, and the harshness of his voice was a lonely token of hopefulness to me. "Or else he's a blacker Judas than he has even confessed, and hopes to become viceroy after the conquest. See you not, 'tis more than the wish for land which'll force the Wersgorix to overrun our planet. 'Tis the fact that our race has proven itself mortally dangerous. As yet, men are helpless at home. But given a few centuries to prepare, men might well build their own spaceships and overwhelm the universe."

"The Wersgorix have suffered in this war," I argued feebly. "They'll need time to regain what they have lost, even if our allies surrender all occupied worlds. They might very likely find it expedient to leave Terra alone for a hundred years or so."

"Till we're safely dead?" Sir Roger nodded heavily. "Aye, there's the great temptation. The real bribe. Yet would we not burn in hell, if we thus broke faith with unborn children?"

"It may be the best we can do for our race," I said. "Whatever lies beyond our own power is in the charge of God."

"But no, no, no." He twisted his hands together. "I can't. Better to die now like men. . . . Yet Catherine—"

After another stillness, I said, "It may not be too late to dissuade Sir Owain. No soul is irredeemably lost while this life remains. You could recall his honor, and point out to him how foolish it is to rely on Wersgor promises, and offer him forgiveness and great position—"

"And the use of my wife?" he jeered.

But in a moment: "It may be. I'd far liefer spill his evil brains. But perhaps . . . aye, perhaps a talk . . . I would even try to humble myself. Will you aid me, Brother Parvus? I must not curse him to his face. Will you strengthen my spirit?"

Chapter XXI

The next evening, we departed New Avalon.

Sir Roger and I went alone, in a tiny unarmed space lifeboat. We ourselves were but little stronger. I had my cassock and rosary as always: no more. He was clad in a yeoman's doublet and hose, though he wore sword and dagger and his gilt spurs were on his boots. His big form sat the pilot chair as it were a saddle, but his eyes, turned heavenward, were full of winter.

We had told our captains that this was only a short flight to view some special thing Sir Owain had fetched. The camp sensed a lie and rumbled with unease. Red John broke two quarterstaffs before he restored order. It seemed to me as I embarked that our enterprise was suddenly rusted. Men sat so quiet. It was a windless evening, our banners drooped on their staffs, and I noticed how faded and torn they were.

Our boat split the blue sky and entered blackness, like Lucifer expelled. Briefly I glimpsed a battleship, patrolling in orbit, and would have been much comforted to have those great guns at my back. But we must take only this helpless splinter. Sir Owain had made that clear, when we talked a second time along the far-speaker beam. "If you wish, de Tourneville, we'll receive you for a parley. But you must come alone, in a plain lifeboat, and unarmed. . . . Oh, very well, you can have your friar, too. . . . I shall tell you what orbit to assume. At a certain point thereof, my ship will meet you. If my telescopes and detectors show any sign of treachery on your part, I'll go straight to Wersgorixan instead."

We accelerated outward through a silence that thickened. Once I ventured to say, "If you two can be reconciled, it will put heart back in our people. I think then they would be truly invincible."

"Catherine and I?" barked Sir Roger.

"Why, I-I-I meant you and Sir Owain—" I stammered. But the truth opened up before me: I had indeed been thinking of the lady. Owain was nothing in himself. Sir Roger was the one on whom our whole fate rested. Yet he could not continue much longer, sundered from her who possessed his soul.

She, and the children they had had together, were the reason he came so meekly to beg Owain's indulgence.

Outward and outward we fled. The planet shrank to a tarnished coin behind us. I had not felt so alone before, not even when we were first borne from our Earth.

But at last a few of the many stars were obscured. I saw the lean black form of the spaceship grow, as it matched velocities. We could have tossed a bombshell by hand and destroyed it. But Sir Owain knew well we would never do that, while Catherine and Robert and Matilda were aboard. Presently a magnetic grapnel clanked against our hull. The ships drew together, portal to portal, a cold kiss. We opened our own gates and waited.

Branithar himself stepped through. Victory flamed in him. He recoiled when he saw Sir Roger's glaive and misericord. "You were to have no weapons!" he rasped.

"Oh? Oh, aye. Aye." The baron looked dully down at the blades. "I never thought ... they're like my spurs, insignia of what I am ... naught more."

"Give them over," said Branithar.

Sir Roger unbelted both and handed them to the Wersgor in their sheaths. Branithar passed them to another blue and searched our bodies himself. "No hidden guns," he decided. I felt my cheeks burn at the insult, but Sir Roger hardly seemed to notice. "Very well," said Branithar, "follow me."

We went down a corridor to the salon cabin. Sir Owain sat behind a table of inlaid wood. He himself was somber in black velvet, but jewels flashed on the hand which covered a fire-gun laid in front of him. Lady Catherine wore a gray gown and wimple. She had overlooked a stray lock of hair, which fell across her brow like smoldering fire.

Sir Roger halted just within the cabin door. "Where are the children?" he said.

"They are in my bedchamber with the maidservants." His wife spoke like a machine. "They are well."

"Be seated, sire," urged Sir Owain glibly. His gaze flickered about the room. Branithar had lain the sword and dagger down by him, and stood on his right hand. The other Wersgor, and a third one who had waited here, stood with folded arms by the entrance, just behind us. I took them to be the physician and navigator which had been mentioned; the two gunners must be at their turrets, the pilot by his controls, in case aught went amiss. Lady Catherine stood, a waxen image, against the rear wall to Owain's left.

"You bear no grudges, I trust," said the recreant. "All's fair in love and war."

Catherine lifted a hand to protest. "In war only." She could scarce be heard. The hand fell down again.

Sir Roger and I kept our feet. He spat on the deck.

Owain reddened. "Look you," he exclaimed, "let's have no cant about broken vows. Your own position is more than doubtful. You've arrogated to yourself the right of creating noblemen out of peasants and serfs, disposing of fiefs, dealing with foreign kings. Why, you'd make yourself king if you could! What then of your pledges to sovereign Edward?"

"I've done naught to his harm," Sir Roger answered, shaken of voice. "If ever I find Terra, I'll add my conquests to his domain. Until then, we must manage somehow, and have no choice but establish our own feudality."

"That may have been the case hitherto," Sir Owain admitted. His smile returned. "But you should thank me, Roger, that I've lifted this necessity from you. We can go back home!"

"As Wersgor cattle?"

"I think not. But do be seated, you two. I shall have wine and cakes brought. You're my guests now, you know."

"Nay. I'll not break bread with you."

"Then you'll starve to death," said Sir Owain merrily.

Roger became like stone. I noticed for the first time that Lady Catherine wore a holster but that it was empty. Owain must have gotten her weapon on some pretext. Now he alone was armed.

He turned grave as he read our expressions. "My lord," he said, "when you offered to come parley, you could not expect me to refuse such a chance. You'll remain with us."

Catherine stirred. "Owain, no!" she cried. "You

never told me—you said he'd be free to leave this ship
if—"

He turned his fine profile to her view and said
gently:

"Think, my lady. Was it not your highest wish, to
save him? But you wept, fearing his pride would never
let him yield. Now he is a prisoner. Your wish is
granted. All the dishonor is on myself. I bear that
burden lightly, since 'tis for my lady's dear sake."

She trembled so I could see it. "I had no part in
this, Roger," she pleaded. "I never imagined—"

Her husband did not look at her. His voice chopped
hers off. "What d' you plan, Montbelle?"

"This new situation has given me new hopes,"
answered the other knight. "I confess I was never
overly joyed at thought of bargaining with the Wersgorix. Now 'tis not needful. We can go directly home.
The weapons and chests of gold aboard this vessel will
win me as much as I care to possess."

Branithar, the only nonhuman there who understood his English, barked: "Hoy, what of me and my
friends here?"

Owain answered coolly, "Why should you not accompany us? Without Sir Roger de Tourneville, the
English cause must soon collapse, so you'll have done
your duty to your own people. I've studied your way
of thinking—a particular place means nothing to you.
We'll pick up some females of your race along the
way. As my loyal vassals, you can win as much power
and land on Terra as anywhere else; your descendants
will share the planet with mine. True, you sacrifice a
certain amount of wonted social intercourse, but on
the other hand, you gain a degree of liberty your own
government never allowed you."

He had the weapons. Yet I think Branithar yielded
to the argument itself, and that his slow mumble of
agreement was honest.

"And us?" breathed Lady Catherine.

"You and Roger shall have your estate in England," pledged Sir Owain. "I'll add thereto one at Winchester."

Perhaps he was also honest. Or perhaps he thought, once he was the overlord of Europe, he could do as he wished with her husband and herself. She was too shaken to foresee the latter chance. I saw her suddenly enclouded with dream. She faced Sir Roger, smiling and weeping. "My love, we can go home again!"

He glanced at her, once. "But what of the folk we led hither?" he asked.

"Nay, I cannot risk taking them with us." Sir Owain shrugged. "They're lowborn anyway."

Sir Roger nodded. "Ah," he said. "So."

Once more he looked at his wife. Then he kicked backward. The spur of knighthood struck into the belly of the Wersgor behind him. He ripped downward.

Falling with the same motion, he rolled across the deck. Sir Owain yelled and leaped up. His fire gun blasted the air. It missed. The baron was too quick, reached upward, seized the other stupefied Wersgor and pulled him down on top. The second fire blast struck that living shield.

Sir Roger heaved the corpse before him, rising and advancing in one gigantic surge of motion. Owain had time for a last shot, which charred the dead flesh. Then Roger threw the body across the table, into the other man's face.

Owain went down beneath it. Sir Roger snatched for his sword. Branithar had already put a hand on it. Sir Roger got the dagger instead. It flared from the sheath. I heard the *thunk* as he drove it through Branithar's hand, into the table, to the very hilt.

"Wait there for me!" snarled Sir Roger. He drew the sword. "Haro! God send the right!"

Sir Owain had scrambled free and risen, still clutching the gun. I found myself a-pant just across the table from him. He aimed squarely at the baron's midriff.

I promised the saints many candles and smacked my rosary across the traitor's wrist. He howled. The gun fell from his hand and skidded across the table. Sir Roger's great glaive whistled. Owain was barely fast enough to dodge. The edged steel crashed into the wood. A moment Sir Roger must struggle to free it. The fire gun lay on the deck. I dove for it. So did Lady Catherine, who had dashed around the table. Our brows met. When my wits came back, I was sitting up and Roger was chasing Owain out the door.

Catherine screamed.

Roger stopped as if noosed. She rose in a swirl of garments. "The children, my lord! They're aft, in the bedchamber—where the extra weapons are—"

He cursed and sped out. She followed. I picked myself up, a trifle groggily, the gun which they had both forgotten in my grasp. Branithar bared teeth at me. He tugged against the knife that pinioned him, but only made the blood run faster. I judged him safely held. My attention was elsewhere. The Wersgor whom my master had disemboweled was still alive, but would not remain so for long. A moment I hesitated . . . where did my duty lie, to my lord and his lady or to a dying heathen? . . . I bent above the contorted blue face. "Father," he gasped. I know not who, or Who, he called upon, but I led him through such poor rites as the circumstances allowed and held him while he died. I pray he may at least have won to Limbo.

Sir Roger came back, wiping his sword. He grinned all over, I have rarely seen such joy in a man. "The little wolf!" he whooped. "Aye, Norman blood is ever easy to tell!"

"What happened?" I asked, rising in my soiled raiment.

"Owain didn't make for the arms chest after all," Sir Roger told me. "He must have turned forward instead, to the control turret. But the other crewmen, the gunners, had heard the fight. Judging the chance ripe and the need clear, they went to equip themselves. I saw one of them pass through the boudoir door. The other was at his heels, armed with a long wrench. I fell upon him with my sword, but he fought well and it took a while to get him slain. Meantime Catherine pursued the first and fought him barehanded till he struck her down. Those chickenheaded maidservants did naught but cower and scream, as expected. But then! Listen, Brother Parvus! My son Robert opened the weapon chest, took forth a gun and plugged that Wersgor as neatly as Red John could have. Oh, the little devil-cub!"

My lady entered. Her braids hung loose, and one fair cheek was purpled with a bruise. But she said as impersonally as any sergeant reporting an assignment of pickets: "I quieted the children down."

"Poor tiny Matilda," murmured her husband. "Was she very much frightened?"

Lady Catherine looked indignant. "They both wanted to come fight!"

"Wait here," he said. "I'll go deal with Owain and the pilot."

She drew a shaken breath. "Must I forever hide away when my lord goes into peril?"

He stopped still and looked upon her. "But I thought—" he began, oddly helpless.

"That I betrayed you merely to win home again? Aye." She stared at the deck. "I think you'll forgive me for that long ere I can ever forgive myself. Yet I did what seemed best . . . for you, too. . . . I was confused. 'Twas like a fever dream. You should not have left me alone so long, my lord. I missed you too much."

Very slowly he nodded. " 'Tis I who must beg pardon," he said. "God grant me years enough to become worthy of you."

Clasping her shoulders: "But remain here. 'Tis

needful you guard yon blueface. If I should kill Owain and the pilot—"

"Do that!" she cried in upsurging fury.

"I'd liefer not," he said with the same gentleness as he used toward her. "Looking upon you, I can understand him so well. But—if worst come to worst—Branithar can guide us home. So watch him."

She took the gun from me and sat down. The nailed captive stood rigid with defiance.

"Come, Brother Parvus," said Sir Roger. "I may need your skill with words."

He carried his sword and had thrust a fire gun from the weapon chest into his belt. We made our way along a corridor, up a ramp, and so to the entrance of the contol turret. Its door was shut, locked from within.

Sir Roger beat upon it with the pommel of his glaive. "You two in there!" he shouted. "Yield yourselves!"

"And if we do not?" Owain's voice drifted faintly through the panels.

"If naught else," said Roger starkly, "I'll wreck the engines and depart in my boat, leaving you adrift. But see here: I've rid myself of anger. Everything has ended for the best, and we shall indeed go home— *after* these stars have been made safe for Englishmen. You and I were friends once, Owain. Give me your hand again. I swear no harm shall come to you."

Silence lay heavy.

Until the man behind the door said: "Aye. You were never one to break an oath, were you? Very well, come on through, Roger."

I heard the bolt click down. The baron put his hand to the door. I know not what impelled me to say, "Wait, sire," and shove myself before him with unheard-of ill manners.

"What is it?" He blinked, bemused in his gladness.

I opened the door and stepped over the threshold. Two iron bars smashed down on my head.

The rest of this adventure must needs be told from hearsay, for I was not to come to my senses for a week. I toppled in blood, and Sir Roger thought me slain.

The moment they saw it was not the baron they had gotten, Owain and the pilot attacked him. They were armed with two unscrewed stanchions, as long and heavy as swords. Sir Roger's blade flashed. The pilot threw up his club. The blade glanced off in a shower of sparks. Sir Roger howled so the walls echoed. "*You murderers of innocence—*" His second blow knocked the bar out of a numbed hand. At his third, the blue head sprang from its shoulders and bounced down the ramp.

Catherine heard the uproar. She went to the door of the salon and looked forward, as if terror could sharpen her eyes to pierce the walls between. Branithar set his teeth together. He seized the misericord with his free hand. Muscles jumped forth in his shoulders. Few men could have drawn that blade, but Branithar did.

My lady heard the noise and whirled. Branithar was rounding the table. His right hand hung torn, astream with blood, but the knife gleamed in his left.

She raised her gun. "Back!" she yelled.

"Put that down," he said scornfully. "You'd never use it. You never saw enough stars at Terra, with wise enough vision. If anything goes wrong in the bows, I am your only way home."

She looked into the eyes of her husband's enemy, and shot him dead. Then she ran toward the turret.

Sir Owain Montbelle had scampered back into that chamber. He could not fend off the sheer fury of Sir Roger's assault. The baron drew his gun. Owain snatched up a book and held it before his breast.

"Have a care!" he panted. "This is the ship's log. It has the notes on Terra's position. There are no others."

"You lie. There's Branithar's mind." Nonetheless, Sir Roger thrust the gun back in his belt as he stalked forward. "I'm sorry to outrage clean steel with your blood. For you killed Brother Parvus and you're going to die."

Owain poised. His stanchion was a clumsy weapon. But he raised his arm and hurled it. Struck across the brow, Sir Roger lurched backward. Owain sprang, snatched the gun from the stunned man's belt, and dodged a feeble sword-slash. He scuttled clear, yelling his triumph. Roger stumbled toward him. Owain took aim.

Catherine appeared in the door. Her gun flamed. The book of her journey vanished in smoke and ash. Owain screamed in anguish. Coldly, she fired again, and he fell.

She flung herself into Roger's arms and wept. He comforted her. Yet I wonder which of them gave the most strength to the other.

Afterward he said ruefully: "I fear we've managed ill. Now the way home is indeed lost."

"It doesn't matter," she whispered. "Where you are, there is England."

Epilogue

A noise of trumpets and cloven air broke loose. The captain laid the typescript down and pressed an intercom button. "What's going on?" he snapped.

"That eight-legged seneschal up at the castle finally got hold of his boss, sir," answered the voice of the sociotech. "As near as I can make out, the planetary duke was out on safari, and it took all this while to locate him. He uses a whole continent for his hunting preserve. Anyhow, he's just now arriving. Come see the show. A hundred antigrav aircraft—good Lord!—the ones that've landed are disgorging horsemen!"

"Ceremonial, no doubt. Just a minute and I'll be there." The captain glared at the typescript. He had read about halfway through it. How could he talk intelligently to this fantastic overlord without some inkling of what had really developed out here?

He skimmed hastily, page after page. The chronicle of the Wersgor Crusade was long and thunderous. Suffice it to read the conclusion, how King Roger I was crowned by the Archbishop of New Canterbury, and reigned for many fruitful years.

But what had *happened?* Oh, sure, one way or another the English won their battles. Eventually they acquired enough actual strength to be independent of their leader's luck and cunning. But their society! How could even their language, let alone their institutions, have survived contact with old and sophisticated civilizations? Hang it, why had the sociotech translated this long-winded Brother Parvus at all, unless some significant data were included? . . . Wait. Yes. A passage near the end caught the captain's eye. He read:

". . . I have remarked that Sir Roger de Tourneville established the feudal system on newly conquered worlds given into his care by the allies. Some latter-day mockers of my noble master have implied he did this only because he knew nothing better to do. I refute this. As I said before, the collapse of Wersgorixan was not unlike the collapse of Rome, and similar problems found a similar answer. His advantage lay in having that answer ready to hand, the experience of many Terrestrial centuries.

"To be sure, each planet was a separate case requiring separate treatment. However, most of them had certain important things in common. The native populations were eager to follow the behest of us, their liberators. Quite apart from gratitude, they were poor ignorant folk, their own civilizations long ago obliterated; they needed guidance in all things. By embracing the Faith, they proved they had souls. This forced our English clergy to ordain converts in great haste. Father Simon found texts of Scripture and the Church Fathers to support this practical necessity—indeed, while he himself never claimed so, it would seem that the veritable God consecrated him a bishop by sending him so far out *in partibus infidelium.* Once this is granted, it follows that he did not exceed his authority in planting the seed of our own Catholic church. Of course, in his day we were always careful to speak of the Archbishop of New Canterbury as 'our' Pope, or the 'popelet,' to remind us that this was a mere agent of the true Holy Father, whom we could not find. I deplore the carelessness of the younger generations in this matter of titles.

"Oddly enough, no few Wersgorix soon came to accept the new order. Their central government had always been a distant thing to them, a mere collector of taxes and enforcer of arbitrary laws. Many a blueskin found his imagination captured by our rich ceremonial and by a government of individual nobles whom he could meet face to face. Moreover, by loyally serving these overlords, he might hope to regain an estate, or even a title. Of the Wersgorix who have repented their sins and become valuable Christian Englishmen, I need only mention our one-time foe Huruga, whom all this world of Yorkshire honors as Archbishop William.

"But there was nothing disingenuous in Sir Roger's proceedings. He never betrayed his allies, as some have charged. He dealt with them shrewdly, but except for the necessary concealment of our true origin (which mask he dropped as soon as we had waxed strong enough not to fear exposure) he was above-board. It was not his fault that God always favors the English.

"Jairs, Ashenkoghli, and Pr?°tans fell in with his proposals readily enough. They had no real concept of empire. If they could have whatever planets without natives we seized, they were quite happy to leave us humans the immensely troublesome task of governing that larger number where a slave population existed. They turned hypocritical eyes away from the often bloody necessities of such government. I am sure that many of their politicians secretly rejoiced that each new responsibility of this sort thinned out the force of their enigmatic associate; for he must create a duke and lesser gentility for it, then leave that small garrison to train the aborigines. Uprisings, internecine war, Wersgor counter-attacks, reduced these tiny cadres still further. Having little military tradition of their own, the Jairs, Ashenkoghli and Pr?°tans did not realize how those cruel years welded bonds of loyalty between native peasants and English aristocrats. Also, being somewhat effete, they did not foresee how lustily humans would breed.

"So in the end, when all these facts were pikestaff plain, it was too late. Our allies were still only three nations, each with its own language and way of life. Springing up around them were a hundred races, united in Christendom, the English tongue, and the English crown. Even if we humans had wished, we could not have changed this. Indeed, we were about as surprised as anyone.

"As proof that Sir Roger never plotted against his allies, consider how easily he could have overrun them in his old age, when he ruled the mightiest nation ever seen among these stars. But he leaned backward to be generous. It was not his doing that their own younger generation, awestruck by our successes, began more and more to imitate our ways. . . ."

The captain put the pages aside and hurried out to the main airlock entrance. The ramp had been let down, and a red-haired human giant was striding up to greet him. Fantastically clad, bearing a florid ornamental sword, he also carried a businesslike blast gun. Behind him an honor guard of riflemen in Lincoln green stood at attention. Over their heads fluttered a banner with the arms of a cadet branch of the great Hameward family.

The captain's hand was engulfed in a hairy ducal paw. The sociotech translated a distorted English: "At last! God be praised, they've finally learned to build spaceships on Old Earth! Welcome, good sir!"

"But why did you never find us . . . er . . . your

grace?" stammered the captain. When it had been translated, the duke shrugged and answered:

"Oh, we searched. For generations every young knight went looking for Earth, unless he chose to look for the Holy Grail. But you know how bloody many suns there are. And even more toward the center of the galaxy—where we encountered still other starfaring peoples. Commerce, exploration, war, everything drew us inward, away from this thinly starred spiral arm. You realize this is only a poor outlying province you've come upon. The King and the Pope dwell away off in the Seventh Heaven.... Finally the quest petered out. In past centuries, Old Earth has become little more than a tradition." His big face beamed. "But now it's all turned topsy-turvy. *You* found *us!* Most wonderful! Tell me at once, has the Holy Land been liberated from the paynim?"

"Well," said Captain Yeshu haLevy, who was a loyal citizen of the Israeli Empire, "yes."

"Too bad. I'd have loved a fresh crusade. Life's been dull since we conquered the Dragons ten years ago. They say, however, that the royal expeditions to the Sagittarian star clouds have turned up some very promising planets— But see here! You must come over to the castle. I'll entertain you as best as I can, and outfit you for the trip to the King. That's tricky navigation, but I'll furnish you with an astrologer who knows the way."

"Now what did he say?" asked Captain haLevy, when the bass burble had stopped.

The sociotech explained.

Captain haLevy turned fire color. "No astrologer is going to touch my ship!"

The sociotech sighed. He'd have a lot of work to do in the coming years.

A SIMPLE SEER

In a display he had never before witnessed, the Stone threw off rays of red and purple light, erupting like gobbets of liquid rock and sparks from the vent of a volcano. Amnet felt the heat against his face. At the focus of the rays was something bright and golden, like a ladle of molten metal held up to him. Without moving, he felt himself pitching forward, drawn down by a pull that was separate from gravity, separate from distance, space, and time. The heat grew more intense. The light more blinding. The angle of his upper body slid from the perpendicular. He was burning. He was falling. . . .

Amnet shook himself.

The Stone, still nestled in the sand, was an inch from his face. Its surface was dark and opaque. The fire among the twigs had burned out. The alembic was clear of smoke, with a puddle of blackened gum at its bottom.

Amnet shook himself again.

What did a vision of the end of the world portend?

And what could a simple aromancer do about it?

MICHAEL FLYNN

IN THE COUNTRY OF THE BLIND

**What if it were all a plot?
What if there really *were* a secret conspiracy
running things behind the scenes ... and
they were incompetent?**

It is a little-known fact that over a hundred years ago
an English scientist-mathematician named Charles
Babbage invented a mechanical computer that was
nearly as powerful as the "electronic brains" of the
1950s. The history books would have it that it was
unworkable, an interesting dead-end.

The history books lie. In reality, the Babbage Machine
was a success whose existence was hidden from view
by a society dedicated to the development of a "secret
science" that could guide the human race away from
war and toward a better destiny.

But as the decades passed their goals were perverted—
and now they apply their knowledge to install themselves
as the secret rulers of the world. Can they do it? Even
though their methods are imperfect, unless they are
stopped their success is assured. *In the Country of
the Blind*, the one-eyed man is King. . . .